The CRUCIAL REVELATION of LIFE in the SCRIPTURES

WITNESS LEE

Living Stream Ministry
Anaheim, California • www.lsm.org

First Edition, December 1987.

ISBN 978-0-87083-372-4

Published by

Living Stream Ministry
2431 W. La Palma Ave., Anaheim, CA 92801 U.S.A.
P. O. Box 2121, Anaheim, CA 92814 U.S.A.

Printed in the United States of America

12   13   14   15   16   /   12   11   10   9   8   7   6

CONTENTS

PREFACE

This book is composed of messages given by Brother Witness Lee in the summer of 1969 in Los Angeles, California.

CHAPTER ONE

LIFE AS SEEN IN GENESIS 1

Scripture Reading: Gen. 1:1-31

THE EARTH BECOMING WASTE AND EMPTINESS

Genesis 1, strictly speaking, is not a record of creation. This is an improper concept. Genesis 1 is a record of life. When I was young, I was taught that verse 1 was the subject of this entire chapter. However, verse 2 begins with the conjunction *but*. This conjunction proves that verse 1 is not the subject but just the beginning of the record. Verse 1 says, "In the beginning God created the heavens and the earth." Verse 2 continues, "But the earth became waste and emptiness, and darkness was on the surface of the deep, and the Spirit of God was brooding upon the surface of the waters." The Hebrew word for *became* is the same word used in Genesis 19:26, which says that Lot's wife became a pillar of salt. Lot's wife was a woman, but she became something else. The earth was originally created by God in a good form, but it became without form; it became waste and emptiness. Isaiah 45:18 tells us that God did not create the earth "waste." This is the same Hebrew word as in Genesis 1:2. God did not create the earth waste, but it became waste. This was due to the rebellion of Satan, which is recorded in Isaiah 14 (vv. 9-14) and Ezekiel 28 (vv. 12-18). Due to Satan's rebellion, the whole universe was judged by God, and through that judgment the earth became waste and emptiness.

In Genesis 1:2 there are four words describing the desolation of the earth under God's judgment: *waste, emptiness, darkness,* and *deep.* The earth became waste and emptiness, and darkness was on the surface of the deep. On the surface of the earth was the deep, and on the surface of the deep was darkness. This tells us that there was no life, but death. The earth becoming waste and emptiness with darkness on the surface of the deep is a picture of death.

THE BROODING SPIRIT

With this background of death, the Scripture continues, "The Spirit of God was brooding upon the surface of the waters" (v. 2). The word for *brood* is the same word as *hovers* in Deuteronomy 32:11. This verse says that God is like an eagle who spreads his wings and hovers over his young. The Spirit of God was brooding, stretching out His wings, over the death situation for the purpose of producing life. The brooding of a hen over eggs is to produce some living things. In the Bible the Spirit of God is first mentioned as the brooding Spirit. This brooding of the Spirit indicates that Genesis 1 is not merely a record of God's creation but a record of life. The Spirit of God was brooding over the death waters for the producing of life.

GOD'S WORK OF RESTORATION AND FURTHER CREATION FOR THE PRODUCING OF LIFE

Genesis 1:3 says, "God said, Let there be light; and there was light." Light comes in to produce life. Where darkness is, there is death. Where light is, there is life. In Genesis 1 light came in mainly for life, not for creation. Genesis 1 is not mainly a record of creation but a record of life. Verse 4 says, "God saw that the light was good, and God separated the light from the darkness." The separation of the light from the darkness is for producing life. When we were saved, the divine light came into us, and that light did a separating, or dividing, work. The things of light were separated from the things of darkness. Light comes in for life, and this light divides, or separates, the positive things from the negative things. Verse 5 says, "God called the light Day, and the darkness He called Night. And there was evening and there was morning, one day." Today we reckon our days from the morning until the evening, but the Bible reckons a day from the evening until the morning. The biblical way is better than the human way. The human way goes down from morning to evening, but the biblical way goes up from evening to morning. There was the evening, but now there is the morning. There was darkness, but now there is light. There was death, but now there is life.

Verses 6 through 8 record what happened on the second day: "God said, Let there be an expanse in the midst of the waters, and let it separate the waters from the waters. And God made the expanse and separated the waters which were under the expanse from the waters which were above the expanse, and it was so. And God called the expanse Heaven." The expanse is a space full of air, separating the waters beneath from the waters above for the producing of life. First, the light was separated from the darkness, and then the air separated the waters beneath from the waters above. Formerly, the waters beneath and the waters above were one, but the air came in to separate these waters, not for creation but for producing life.

On the third day there was a third step of separation. All the waters were gathered together into one place, and the dry land appeared (v. 9). All the waters had to be gathered together so that the land might come out of the death waters. The first step of separation was to separate light from darkness. The second step was to separate the waters under the expanse from the waters above the expanse. Then the third step was to separate the land from the waters under the expanse. Light, air, and land are for the producing of life. After these three steps of separation, different forms of life came out of the land. Verse 11 mentions grass, herbs, and trees. In the vegetable life, grass is the lowest form, and the trees are the highest. The grass, the herbs, and the trees are different kinds of plant or vegetable life, the life without consciousness.

There was the need of some higher life with consciousness. As a result, the higher light was needed. Without the higher light, there cannot be the higher life. Thus, on the fourth day the light became more solid, more substantial. There were two great light-bearers: the greater to rule the day and the lesser to rule the night (v. 16). In addition to these two great light-bearers, there are the stars. On the fourth day the light became intensified. This fourth-day light is for the higher life.

On the fifth day there was the higher life with conscious-ness— the animal life in the death waters and the life that could fly in the air (vv. 20-21). The life that is able to move in the air is a transcendent life and is higher than the life in the death waters.

On the sixth day the earth brought forth all the living creatures. These creatures are mainly of three categories: the cattle, the creeping things, and the animals (v. 24). On the sixth day God made the highest life forms among the animal life. Also on the sixth day there was the highest life, the human life. First there was the plant life, then the animal life, and finally the human life. The human life not only possesses consciousness but also possesses the image of God, the like-ness of God, and is entrusted with the authority of God (v. 26). The highest created life is the human life. Eventually, in Gen-esis 2:9 the highest life is revealed, and that life is the divine life.

In God's restoration and further creation in the universe, everything that God called into being was declared to be "good." On the first day "God saw that the light was good" (1:4). On the third day the dry land appeared, and out from the dry land came the plant life. God also saw that this was good. The land coming out of the death waters was a type of Christ in resurrection. Just as the land appeared on the third day, Christ was resurrected from the death waters on the third day, and all the aspects of life came out of this resur-rected Christ. On the fourth day the sun, moon, and stars became visible, and God saw that this was good. On the fifth day the animal life came into being. God not only said that this was good, but He also blessed the animals that they might be fruitful and multiply. Eventually, in the last verse of Genesis 1, "God saw everything that He had made, and indeed, it was very good." With all the other created items, God only saw that they were good. By the end of Genesis 1, God said "very good" because man was there. Man is a very good item in God's creation because man is the center of God's creation.

God said "very good" because by that time He had a man to
fulfill His purpose by life and in life.

THE HIGHER LIGHT FOR THE HIGHER LIFE

Genesis 1 reveals that the higher light always comes in for
the higher life. On the first day God said, "Let there be light."
Then on the fourth day there was the intensified light.
Finally, on the seventh day there was the biggest light, God
Himself. The starting light was for the unconscious life, the
bigger light was for the conscious life, and the biggest light
was for the divine life. Genesis 1 is such a record of life.

FOUR STEPS OF SEPARATION

We have also pointed out that there were four steps of
separation in Genesis 1: the light was separated from the
darkness, the waters under the expanse were separated from
the waters above the expanse, the land was separated from the
death waters, and on the fourth day the day was separated
from the night. Before the fourth day, the days were not so
solid. On the fourth day God made the greater light-bearer
to rule the day and the lesser light-bearer to rule the night.
Then the day was solidly separated from the night.

The human life came in after the fourth day, after all the
four steps of separation. After these steps of separation were
completed, God was able to make man in His image and
according to His likeness. The human life, which has the image
and likeness of God, is the highest created life. God created
man according to His likeness. All the other lives are according to their kind. The human life, however, is not according to
the human kind but according to God's kind.

GOD'S FURTHER CREATION
ACCORDING TO THE ORDER OF LIFE

God created all things according to the order of life. The
plant life, the animal life, the human life, and the divine life
are the four levels of life in Genesis 1 and 2. These levels of
life are mentioned in order from the lowest to the highest.
The different types of plant life and animal life are also mentioned according to degree, from the lowest to the highest.

The lowest level in the plant life is the grass. Then there are the herbs and the trees. In the animal life first there are the fish, and then there are the birds. The human life is a wonderful life because this life resembles God. This is the God-like life, the life according to God's kind, with God's image, with God's likeness, and committed and entrusted with the divine authority to become God's representative on this earth. The human life is the highest among all the created lives. It is only lower than the uncreated life, the divine life.

GOD'S INTENTION

After such a study we can realize that God's intention in Genesis 1 was to show us that His heart's desire is in the matter of life. Eventually, in Genesis 2 the tree of life is presented to the created man. The record of Genesis 1 and 2 leads us to this one point of life. God's intention is that man would take Him in as the divine life. The record of God's creation is so simple because God did not mainly pay attention to all the items and aspects of His creation. That was not God's intention. God focuses on one thing—the matter of life. God's intention from the very beginning was for man to receive Him as the divine life in order that man might become God's expression in this universe.

CHAPTER TWO

LIFE FOR IMAGE AND DOMINION

Scripture Reading: Gen. 1:21, 26-28, 31; Matt. 6:10; Col. 1:15;
Rom. 8:29; 12:2; 2 Cor. 3:18; 1 John 3:2; Luke 10:19; Rev.
2:26-27; Gen. 2:10-12, 18-24

GOD'S DESIRE TO EXPRESS HIMSELF
AND DEAL WITH HIS ENEMY

Life is for the expression of God. There is the need of life
because God's intention is to express Himself, and life is the
means to express God. In creation all the lower lives are for
the higher lives, all the higher lives are for the highest created
life, and this highest life is for the divine life. Man as the highest created life is living to express God. We must remember
that man is according to God's kind. Man is not in his likeness
but in God's likeness. Man is not in his image but in God's
image. James tells us that man uses his tongue not only to
bless the Lord but also to "curse men, who have been made
according to the likeness of God" (3:9). We have to realize that
all men have been made according to the likeness of God, so
we should not despise any man. First Corinthians 11:7 says,
"A man ought not to have his head covered, since he is God's
image and glory." Man was made in God's image (Gen. 1:26) to
express God and glorify Him. We may say that God is our glory,
but this verse says that we are God's glory. We may realize
that God is our glory and may want to experience God as our
glory, but we also have to realize that we are God's glory
because we are going to express God by His life. Without life,
man can never express God. Thus, life is the means for us to
express God. The plant life and the animal life are for the

human life, for us to live for God. The human life, the highest created life, is for the divine life, the uncreated life.

Man was created not only to express God but also to represent God. We have been committed, entrusted, with God's authority. This means that God has authorized us to be His representatives. Thus, we have dominion over all things on earth except God (v. 26). God is above us; we are under God, but we are above everything else. We are above the things in the water, the things on the earth, and the things in the air. Man is the real commander in chief of the land, of the sea, and of the air, and he was made to represent God by life.

God's eternal purpose is to have Himself expressed through the created human life, but Satan came in to frustrate this. He did everything he could to damage God's purpose, to frustrate God from accomplishing His eternal intention. There is a struggle, a war, in the universe between Satan and God. God's direction is toward the expression of Himself, and Satan's direction is against this. Thus, in this universe there are two directions: the divine direction and the satanic direction. These two directions contradict each other. God is going to fulfill His purpose, and Satan is doing everything he can to frustrate God's purpose. This is the unique war and struggle in the entire universe, and this war is also going on within us. Within us there is a struggle between Satan and God. God wants to express Himself through us, and Satan is doing everything to frustrate this.

Before man was created, Satan rebelled against God and ruined and even usurped the earth. In a sense, the right of God on this earth has been robbed by Satan. The earth was and still is, in a sense, under the usurping hand of the enemy (1 John 5:19). There is no problem for God in the heavens, but there is a real problem for God on this earth. This is why the Lord Jesus prayed, "Your will be done, as in heaven, so also on earth" (Matt. 6:10). There is no problem for God's will in heaven, but there is a real problem for God's will on this earth. This is why we need to pray that the Father's will would be done on earth as it is in heaven. The real problem is that Satan today is usurping the earth. The earth is under his usurping hand. This is why God said in Genesis 1 that the life that resembles Him has to conquer the earth, to subdue the earth (v. 28). The earth has to be subdued and conquered because of the rebellion against God on this earth instigated by Satan. The rebellious earth needs to be conquered by man living with God's life. To conquer, to subdue, the earth we need the divine life.

Genesis 1:26 tells us that man was to have dominion "over every creeping thing that creeps upon the earth." Among the creeping things is the serpent. The serpent signifies Satan, the devil, who is the leader of the creeping things (cf. Luke 10:19). To have dominion over the creeping things means to rule over Satan. To conquer means to conquer the rebellion of Satan. Since God is almighty, all powerful, it would be easy for Him to get rid of Satan on His own. But God would not get rid of Satan directly by Himself. God wanted another creature, man, to be used by Him to get rid of Satan. Thus, the human life is the means for God to get rid of Satan.

In His creation of man, God desires to accomplish two things: He wants to express Himself, and He wants to get rid of His enemy, Satan. God uses man to express Himself and to get rid of Satan.

God's Intention for Man
to Express Him in His Image

Genesis 1:26 tells us that man was made in the image of God. On the one hand, the Bible tells us clearly that God is invisible, yet on the other hand, the Bible tells us also that God has an image. In Genesis 1:26 God says, "Let Us make man in Our image," but verse 27 says that God created man "in His own image." Verse 26 uses the plural pronoun *our,* and verse 27 uses the singular pronoun *His,* showing that man was made in the image of the Triune God. Colossians 1:15 tells us that Christ is the image of the invisible God. Thus, man was created according to Christ because Christ is the image of God.

God's intention is that we would be conformed to the image of His Son (Rom. 8:29). Second Corinthians 3:18 tells us that we have to be transformed into the Lord's image from one degree of glory to another degree of glory. We were made in the Triune God's image, which is Christ, and eventually we will become God's image. We have received Christ into us, and He is gradually transforming us into His image. In eternity as the New Jerusalem, all God's redeemed people will be fully conformed to the image of God's Son to express God to the uttermost. Christ is the image of God, so He is the model, the pattern, the mold. When clay or dough is put into a mold, it is conformed to the image of that mold. We were made according to Christ, and we have received Christ into us so that we may actually be transformed and conformed into the image of Christ to eventually express Christ in His image in eternity. In eternity we will be absolutely like Him. First John 3:2 says, "Beloved, now we are children of God, and it has not yet been manifested what we will be. We know that if He is manifested, we will be like Him because we will see Him even as He is." God's purpose will be fulfilled when we are fully transformed and conformed into His image. At that time, we will be fully one with God and fully according to God's kind. We will be God's expression, fully expressing Him in His image.

God's Intention for Man to Represent Him with His Authority

Furthermore, God's intention is for man to represent Him with His authority. He desires that man would reign in His life (Rom. 5:17). After the resurrection the Lord Jesus told the disciples that all authority had been given to Him in heaven and on earth (Matt. 28:18). Because all the authority had been given to Him, Christ as the heavenly King sent His disciples to go and disciple all the nations (v. 19). We as His disciples go with His authority. Christ has given us not only His power but also His authority to rule over Satan. In Luke 10:19 the Lord said, "Behold, I have given you the authority to tread upon serpents and scorpions and over all the power of the enemy, and nothing shall by any means hurt you." Serpents may signify Satan and his angels (Eph. 2:2; 6:11-12); scorpions may signify the demons (Luke 10:17, 20). The disciples subdued their evil power by the authority of the Lord.

One day the overcomers will have the authority to rule

over the earth, just as Christ has such authority. Revelation 2:26-27 says, "He who overcomes and he who keeps My works until the end, to him I will give authority over the nations; and he will shepherd them with an iron rod, as vessels of pottery are broken in pieces, as I also have received from My Father." Psalm 2:8-9 tells us that God gave Christ authority to rule over the nations; here in Revelation 2 Christ gives the same authority to His overcomers. Revelation 20:4-5 tells us that the overcomers are sitting upon thrones, and authority to judge has been given to them. These overcomers reign with Christ for a thousand years. The resurrection of kingship is a reward to the overcomers that they may reign as co-kings with Christ in the millennial kingdom (cf. v. 6). Finally, all God's redeemed will "reign forever and ever" (22:5) as the constituents of the New Jerusalem. To reign forever will be the final blessing to God's redeemed in eternity.

THE ISSUE OF THE FLOW OF LIFE

We have seen that God's desire is for man to be filled with His life so that man might express Him in His image and represent Him with His dominion. God's desire for man to express Him and for man to have dominion over His enemy can be realized only by God's life. Thus, we see in Genesis 2 that God placed man in front of the tree of life with the intention that man would take God as life into himself (vv. 8-9). Genesis 2 also says that a river went forth from Eden to water the garden (v. 10), showing that when we partake of God as life, we are brought into the fellowship, the flow, of this life.

Transformed into Precious Materials
for God's Building

The issue of the flow of life as seen in Genesis 2 is gold, bdellium (a kind of pearl), and onyx stone (vv. 11-12). As we enjoy the Triune God, the flow of the divine life within us, we are transformed into precious materials for God's building in the entire universe. The issue of the flow is transformation and building.

The three precious materials in Genesis correspond to the

three persons of the Godhead. Gold typifies God the Father in His divine nature. When we were saved, we were born of the Father, and the Father's divine nature was imparted into us. We have become partakers of God the Father's divine nature (2 Pet. 1:4).

To consider the significance of pearls, we need to consider how a pearl is formed. First, an oyster is wounded by a particle of sand. This particle lodges in the wound of the oyster, and the oyster secretes its life-juice around the sand to produce a pearl. A particle of sand is changed into a pearl through the process of secretion. This depicts Christ as the living One coming into the death waters, being wounded by us, and secreting His life over us to make us precious pearls for the building of God's eternal expression. Christ was the real, living oyster who came into the death waters. He was wounded for our transgressions, and we believed in His redemptive death. Thus, He was able to secrete His life over us for us to become pearls. On the one hand, we have the blood of Christ to cleanse us, and on the other hand, we have the life of Christ secreting all the time into us and upon us to make us pearls for God's building.

Precious stones are produced through a tremendous amount of pressure and heat. When a black piece of coal is subjected to tremendous amounts of pressure and heat over a period of many years, it will be transformed into a diamond. In a sense, we are like the black coal, and we are under the pressure and in the oven. Job, David, and all the saints who followed the Lord in the way of His heart's desire passed through the heat and pressure so that they could be transformed into precious stones. All the sufferings that Job went through were measured by God. God allowed Satan to go only so far with Job. There was a limit as to what Job would pass through. All of us have to pass through the pressure and the heat. Then we will be transformed into precious stones.

Apart from the Lord we human beings are not stone but vessels of clay. Clay is good only for making bricks, which are pieces of clay that have been burnt. In the Bible the buildings built up by Satan were built with bricks, such as Babel (Gen. 11:3-4) and the storage cities of Egypt (Exo. 1:11, 14). On the other hand, the building built up by God is built with precious stones (1 Cor. 3:12; Rev. 21:19-20). In Matthew 16 when Simon Peter recognized the Lord as the Christ and as the Son of the living God, the Lord changed his name from Simon Bar-jona to Peter, which means "a stone," material for God's building (1 Pet. 2:5). Originally, Simon was a man of clay, but the Lord changed him into a living stone. Eventually, we believers are all the living stones to be transformed into precious stones. How much transformation we need!

The work of the Holy Spirit in our environment is to burn us and press us. Whether we like this or not, we need it, and the Holy Spirit has to do it. The Holy Spirit day by day is burning us and putting some pressure upon us. When a brother gets married, he gets into the oven. The husband becomes the oven to the wife, and the wife becomes the oven to the husband. The wife and the husband burn each other. Furthermore, the husband many times is not a pleasure to the wife but a pressure, and the wife is a real pressure to the husband. When a couple has children, these little ones increase the pressure and the heat. All the married brothers and sisters know what I am talking about. This is the Lord's way to transform us. The Triune God is working within us and on us to transform us into gold, pearls, and precious stones. This transformation is for the preparation of the bride of Christ, for the building up of the church.

The church cannot be built up by doctrinal teachings or by organization. The church can come into being only by the flowing of the divine life that transforms us into gold, pearls, and precious stones. Without the experience and enjoyment of the inner flow of life in the midst of an environment of heat and pressure, we will remain men of clay. Clay is not the proper material for God's heavenly, spiritual, and divine building work. A local church cannot be realized by teaching or by organization. The only way that a local church can be built up is by life. This is why we must stress and focus on the divine life all the time. We must try our best by His mercy and grace to minister life to others. We have to eat the tree of life and drink the river of water of life day after day so that we can be transformed into precious material. What the church needs today is the ministry of life. Life is the only means, the only way, for the church to be built up.

How the Bride of Christ Comes into Being

In Genesis 2 there is the picture of how the bride of Christ comes into being. Before God prepared a bride for Adam, He brought all the animals to Adam, and Adam named each one. But none of these created things matched Adam, and they could not be his counterpart (vv. 19-20). Then God caused a deep sleep to fall upon Adam (v. 21). Adam is a type of Christ (Rom. 5:14), and his sleep is a type of Christ's death. In the Bible sleep means death (1 Cor. 15:18; 1 Thes. 4:13-16; John 11:11-14).

During Adam's sleep, God took one of his ribs from his side. Likewise, when Christ was sleeping on the cross, something came out of His side. John 19:34 tells us that when the soldier pierced His side, out came blood and water. At Adam's time there was no sin, so there was no need of redemption. It was not until Genesis 3 that sin came in. Thus, all that came out of Adam's side was the rib without the blood. However, by the time that Christ was sleeping on the cross, there was the problem of sin. Thus, His death must deal with this sin problem. The blood came out of Christ's side for redemption. Following the blood, the water came out, which is the flowing life to produce the church. This divine, flowing, uncreated life is typified by the rib taken out of Adam's side.

When the Lord Jesus was dying on the cross, two others were dying with Him. Their legs were broken, but when the soldiers came to the Lord Jesus, He was already dead, and there was no need to break His bones. This fulfilled the prophecy that not one of His bones would be broken (John 19:31-33). Thus, the bone taken out of Adam's side signifies the Lord's unbroken, unbreakable, resurrection life. His resurrection life is unbreakable. The rib taken out of Adam signifies the resurrection life, and God built a woman with the rib of Adam. Now God builds up the church with the resurrection life of Christ. Just as Eve was a part of Adam, so the church is a part of Christ. Eve was bone of Adam's bones and flesh of Adam's flesh. Today we as the church are a part of Christ

(Eph. 5:30-32). This marvelous revelation can be seen by comparing Genesis 2, John 19, and Ephesians 5.

When we received the Lord Jesus, He came into us as the resurrection life, the unbreakable life. It is this life that transforms us. This life is the tree of life, the river of life, the very life that supplies us and that flows within us to transform us. Day by day as we enjoy this flowing, divine, uncreated, unbreakable life, we are being transformed. This transformation is mentioned and revealed in Romans 12:2 and 2 Corinthians 3:18. As we are being transformed, we are also being built into the church to be the bride to satisfy Christ as His counterpart. At the end of Genesis 2 is Eve, and at the end of the entire Bible is the New Jerusalem, which is the ultimate Eve, the ultimate consummation of the universal bride built up with precious materials produced by the resurrection life of Christ.

The life seen in Genesis 2 is the flowing life, the transforming life, and the building life. This life flows within us, transforms us, and eventually builds us up as the bride of Christ. This bride, the New Jerusalem, will fulfill the two aspects of the purpose of God. First, the New Jerusalem will be the full expression of God in God's full image (Rev. 21:11; cf. 4:3). Second, this New Jerusalem will subdue the enemy, conquer the earth, and exercise God's authority over the entire universe, especially over the creeping things (22:5; 21:15; cf. v. 8; 20:10, 14-15). God's dominion will be realized on the whole earth through the New Jerusalem. Thus, God's purpose is fully fulfilled by the New Jerusalem, which is the result, the issue, the ultimate consummation of life. What we believers need is life, and this life is nothing less than the Triune God Himself, the Father in the Son and the Son as the Spirit. May we all be brought into the enjoyment and experience of this flowing, transforming, and building life to be prepared as the bride that will bring Christ back.

CHAPTER THREE

THE LAMB, THE MANNA, AND
THE PRODUCE OF THE LAND FOR EATING

Scripture Reading: Exo. 12:2-11; 13:4; 16:13b-15, 31, 35; Num. 11:7-8; Josh. 5:10-12

Genesis is a book of creation, and Exodus is a book of redemption. We have seen in the first two chapters of Genesis that from the very beginning God's intention was that man would partake of the tree of life. The tree of life signifies God Himself as life to us in the form of food. The more that we eat of Him, enjoy Him, partake of Him as our life, the more He will be assimilated into us to be one with us in the way of mingling. In Genesis 3 it is recorded that man fell. The evil one came into the man that God created for His purpose, so man was corrupted, ruined. There is a real problem with man, so there is the need of deliverance. This is why the book of Exodus is needed.

From Genesis 3 to Exodus 12 is a long period with a long history. In this long period of time, the fall of man is recorded. This fall started from Adam and went on to the children of Israel. The end of Genesis shows us where man was. Genesis 50:26 tells us that man ended up "in a coffin in Egypt." This was the place where man fell. In the beginning God created the heavens and the earth, and then God created man in His own image. God placed this man in front of the tree of life with the intention that man would partake of this tree. But man fell and fell and fell until he ended up "in a coffin in Egypt." The first verse of Genesis says, "In the beginning God created...," and the last verse says that man was now "in a coffin in Egypt." Because man was now in a coffin in Egypt, he needed redemption, deliverance. This is why the book of Exodus is needed.

THE LAMB

The first part of Exodus tells us that man was in slavery working for Satan. Pharaoh, who typifies God's enemy Satan, forced the children of Israel to build two storage cities for him (1:11). This work was a work of death, a dead work. In God's eyes the children of Israel were working in a coffin in Egypt, so they needed deliverance. Exodus 12 tells us how God came in to deliver His people from the bondage of His enemy. In Exodus 12 God did not present the children of Israel with the tree of life but with a lamb. The tree of life was changed to the lamb because man had become fallen.

The Need of Life and Redemption

In the book of Exodus God came in to recover man, who had been put into a coffin in Egypt. Before we got saved, we also were in a coffin in Egypt. The Lord came to us when we were in such a situation, and He presented Himself to us as the Lamb of God. Since man fell, the tree of life was not in itself adequate to deliver man. To solve the problem of the fall of man, both life and redemption are needed. Redemption recovers the fallen people, and life keeps the original purpose of God. We all need to say, "Hallelujah for the Lamb," because the Lamb fulfills the purpose of redemption and the purpose of life. The Lamb affords us both blood and meat. The blood of the Lamb is for redemption (vv. 7, 13), and the meat of the Lamb is for life (vv. 4, 8-11). God did not give up His original purpose, but because of man's fall, something else had been added. Life is not adequate, and there is now the need of redemption, so the tree of life became the Lamb.

Both the Lamb and the tree are in the Gospel of John. The Gospel of John tells us that in the beginning was the Word (1:1a), the Word was God (v. 1b), the Word became flesh (v. 14), and this Word become flesh, this God-man, is the Lamb of God who takes away the sin of the world (v. 29). John 15 unveils the vine tree, which is the tree of life that supplies life. The Lamb is Christ for redemption, and the tree is Christ for life.

Abib—A New Beginning

The Lord told Moses and Aaron that they had to make the month of their redemption the beginning of months, the first of the months of the year to them (Exo. 12:2). This month in which they came out of Egypt was the month of Abib (13:4). Originally, this month was the seventh month, but the Lord made it to be the first month of the year, the beginning of all the months. In the beginning God created, but what God had created was put into a coffin in Egypt. Thus, there was the need of another beginning. The beginning in Genesis 1 was buried in a coffin, but in Exodus 12 God made another beginning. The first beginning is in Genesis 1, and that beginning was for creation. The second beginning is in Exodus 12, and this beginning was for redemption. The first beginning was for creation with the purpose of life. The second beginning was for redemption with the same purpose of life. God has the same purpose with two beginnings. We all need to realize that we have had two beginnings. When we received the Lord, we had another beginning.

This first month of the year was called Abib. *Strong's Exhaustive Concordance* tells us that this word means a young ear of grain or green ears of corn. The ears of corn that are young, green, and tender point to a new beginning. *Young's Analytical Concordance* tells us that *Abib* refers to something sprouting and budding. This is the start of life. When some people ask me what the date of my birth is, I would like to tell them that my birthday is Abib. Abib was our beginning. This beginning is not the beginning of creation but the beginning of a new life. Something is sprouting, budding, with the green, young, and tender ears of corn. This signifies new life and also indicates something further than the tree of life. This new life is something budding, something that sprouts, something that produces green, tender, young ears, and something that is growing. We have to learn how to understand the Bible by looking at the pictures in the Old Testament. A picture is better than a thousand words. This second beginning is the beginning of life, and this life is a budding, sprouting life.

The Lamb for Life

The children of Israel were in a coffin in Egypt. Even if they were brought out of Egypt and put into Canaan, they were still dead, without life. They needed to be brought out of the coffin, out of Egypt, and they needed life put into them. The life is signified by the meat of the lamb.

Exodus 12 tells us that the Lord told the children of Israel to prepare the lamb according to each man's eating (v. 4). If a person could eat more, he would have to prepare more of the lamb. This means that the lamb is prepared not according to redemption but according to the life capacity. This is because the lamb is not merely for redemption but more importantly for life. Do you need a bigger portion or a smaller portion of the lamb? You may think that you are so sinful and that your sins are greater than others so you need a bigger Christ. This is a human concept but not the divine concept. The divine concept is that we have to prepare the lamb according to our eating. Christ is allotted to us according to the eating capacity, the life capacity.

Our intention is not to lower down the value of the Lord's redemption, but many Christians stress redemption and forget the matter of life. I heard a number of messages on the passover when I was young. The blood of the Lamb that redeems us and causes God to pass over us was always stressed. This is good and true, but we need to realize that the blood is not the goal. The blood is the procedure to reach the goal. The goal is life. The goal is that we may have the Lamb get into us, that we may have the Lamb within us as our life.

Because we are sinful in the eyes of God, we need the blood. The children of Israel were fallen and sinful like the Egyptians. On the night of the passover, God came to the earth to judge the sinful people. Without the covering of the blood, the children of Israel would be smitten by God in the same way that the Egyptians would. But God gave them the way for Him to pass over them. They needed the covering of the blood, so they killed the lamb according to God's instructions.

They took the blood of the lamb and put it on the two door-posts and on the lintel of their houses (v. 7). Then their houses were sprinkled with the redeeming blood, and they were eating the meat of the lamb within their houses. This means that they were under the covering of the blood. Then God came to judge Egypt and smote everyone who was not under the covering of the blood of the lamb. But God passed over the children of Israel who were under this covering. When the Egyptians were being smitten by God, the children of Israel were enjoying the meat of the lamb under the covering of the blood. Thus, the blood is for the meat; that is, redemption is for life.

Not Eaten Raw or Boiled

Related to the eating of the meat of the lamb, there were a few things that needed to be taken care of. The Lord told the children of Israel that they should not eat the meat when it was raw or boiled. The lamb had to be roasted with fire (v. 9). To be raw indicates no passing through of sufferings, and to be boiled means to suffer something merely under the human hand. The modernists say that Christ's death was only a martyrdom. To them Christ merely suffered the persecution from man. This is what it means for the lamb to be boiled. But to be roasted with fire means to suffer under God's burning judgment. Fire represents God's holy anger. For the lamb to be roasted means that Christ had to be judged by God. Christ suffered not just under the hand of man as a kind of persecution, but under the hand of God as divine punishment, divine judgment. This is the roasting under the divine fire. Christ is not a raw lamb or a lamb boiled with water. Our Lamb, our Christ, is a Lamb roasted under the divine fire. We take this Christ.

One with the Lamb by Eating the Lamb

When I was young, I was always taught that we had to take Christ as our example. Because Christ loves people, we have to imitate Him to love people. Because Christ was nice and humble while He was on this earth, we were taught that we had to be the same way. To imitate Christ in this way is impossible. The best way to follow the Lord is to get Him into us by eating Him. We need to be one with the Lamb by eating the Lamb. Then we will be constituted with the Lamb. God did not tell the children of Israel to slay one lamb for the blood and then to have another lamb that they needed to learn to follow. God told them to slay one lamb, put the blood on the house, and under the covering of this blood eat this slain, roasted lamb. In this way the lamb would be one with the children of Israel, would be in them, and would be their constituent. The thought here is very deep. The Christian life is not a matter of imitating Christ, of following Christ in an outward way. But it is a matter of our eating Christ, receiving Christ into us, and assimilating all that He is into our being.

Eaten with Unleavened Bread
and Bitter Herbs

The children of Israel also had to eat the lamb with unleavened bread with bitter herbs (v. 8). The bread with the herbs signifies that the passover was composed not only of the animal life but also of the vegetable life, the plant life. The tree of life was the plant life, but the lamb is the animal life. The lamb is first for redemption, but after redemption is accomplished and experienced, the lamb becomes the tree of life to give us life.

In John 6 the Lord Jesus told us that He is the bread of life (v. 35). He also told us that His blood is drinkable and that His flesh is eatable (v. 55). In John 6:51 the Lord said that the bread which He will give is His flesh. In John 6 the bread of wheat is also the bread of blood and meat. Christ was the Lamb slain for us, and with the Lamb there is the blood and the meat. Christ also is life to us, so He is the bread of life, the tree of life, the plant life. In John 1 is the Lamb, and in John 15 is the tree of life. Between these two chapters is the bread of life in chapter 6 with blood and meat. On the one hand, Christ is the redeeming life, the animal life, but on the other hand, Christ is the generating life, the plant life. He is the lamb, the animal life, for redeeming and the tree, the plant life, for generating. Thus, there are the matters of redemption and life.

The bread is of the vegetable life and is only for feeding; the flesh is of the animal life and is not only for feeding but also for redeeming. Before the fall of man, the Lord was the tree of life (Gen. 2:9), only for feeding man. After man fell into sin, the Lord became the Lamb (John 1:29), not only for feeding man but also for redeeming man (Exo. 12:4, 7-8, 12-13).

Eating for Moving

Exodus 12 also tells us that the children of Israel ate the lamb with their loins girded, with their sandals on their feet, and with their staff in their hand (v. 11). They did not eat the lamb in a sloppy or a slow way. They ate the lamb in haste. I believe that all of them stood while they ate. Their loins were girded, their sandals were on their feet, and they had a staff in their hand. Suppose they had the blood covering them without the meat for them to eat. God may have given them the commandment to gird their loins, put their sandals on their feet, take their staff, and be in haste to get out of Egypt. If this had been the case, they would have still been hungry. Although they would have had the blood covering them, they would have still been empty within. Without eating, they would not have had the energy to leave Egypt in haste. This picture shows us that the eating of the lamb was for moving. Life is for us to move. They were eating the lamb in a moving way. While they were eating, they were getting ready to get out of Egypt. When we take our meals, we usually sit down and relax. But during the passover, the children of Israel ate in haste because eating was for them to move. This is a new beginning, not of creation but the beginning of redemption for life.

THE MANNA

The record of the history of God's people refers again and again to the matter of eating. After the children of Israel came out of Egypt, the matter of eating was of central importance in the wilderness. They began to eat manna.

A Mystery

The word *manna* in Hebrew means "What is it?" or "What is this?" On the morning when the children of Israel first saw this small, round, white thing on the ground, they did not know what it was. Thus, they asked one another, "What is this?" "What is this?" is the meaning of the word *manna*. We may know what corn and wheat are, but what is this? To the people of the world Christ is manna; that is, He is "what is this?" The professors may know physics, mathematics, history, and geography, but when it comes to Christ, they would ask, "What is this?" Christ is the real manna, the real "what is this?" Christ is the heavenly food on this earth. On this earth there is nothing like manna. Manna, the heavenly Christ as our heavenly food, is a mystery.

The Taste of Honey and Fresh Oil

The manna had the taste of honey and of fresh oil (16:31; Num. 11:8). When we eat the manna, we enjoy the honey and the oil. Oil in the Bible signifies the Spirit. In this manna is the taste of the Spirit and the taste of honey. Honey is the mingling of two lives, the animal life and the vegetable life. The honeybees which produce honey receive the supply from flowers, from the vegetable life. As our manna, Christ has this element of the mingling of the animal life, the redeeming life, with the vegetable life, the generating life. This mingling is our sweet nourishment.

Small and Round

Exodus also tells us that the manna was fine and round (16:14). The fineness or smallness of manna means that it was ready and available to be taken in by God's people. The food taken in by us must be small enough to eat. Anything that is fine, such as fine flour, fine sugar, or fine salt, is ready and available for us to use. The roundness of manna signifies that Christ is eternal, perfect, and full, without beginning or ending. Christ is eternal food with an eternal nature for eternal nourishment without limitation. This eternal food without beginning and without ending is the eternal life.

White and Like Frost

Furthermore, Exodus 16:31 indicates that manna was white. It was clean and pure, without any kind of mixture. Christ as our life and our life supply is so pure, so white. The manna was also like frost (v. 14). Frost is something between dew and snow. Both dew and frost are refreshing. But although dew refreshes, it does not kill germs. Frost, however, does kill germs. The life of Christ is so refreshing, so cooling, and it kills the negative things within us.

Coming with the Dew

The manna also came with the dew in the morning according to Exodus 16:13-14. The dew not only refreshes but also waters. The life, which is Christ, is a watering life. The dew is softer than rain and not as cold as frost.

The Appearance of Bdellium

In Numbers 11:7 we are told that the appearance of manna was like the appearance of bdellium. This means that Christ as our daily life supply is so transparent. Furthermore, the meaning of transformation is implied here. The more we enjoy Christ as our heavenly food, the more we will become transparent and transformed into material for God's building.

Eaten as Bread, Cakes, and Wafers

The manna was eaten as bread (Exo. 16:15), as cakes (Num. 11:8), and as wafers (Exo. 16:31). As our manna, Christ has different aspects and nourishes us in different ways. When we eat Him as our manna, sometimes He tastes like bread, and at other times He tastes like cake or a wafer, which is thin and easy to eat and digest.

Not Legal

Finally, as the manna, Christ is not legal. Numbers 11:8 says, "The people went about and gathered it and ground it between two millstones or beat it in a mortar; then they boiled it in pots and made cakes of it." Christ can be ground, beaten in a mortar, or boiled in pots. If you experience Christ in a certain way, you may make that a legal way. But Christ is not legal. He can be taken and experienced by us in many ways.

The Continuation of the Passover Lamb

We have to realize that manna is the continuation of the passover lamb. The passover lamb was the beginning of the children of Israel's eating, and manna became the continuation of that eating for forty years. Every morning for forty years, wherever they went and wherever they were, manna was there for the children of Israel to eat. This was a real miracle. The fact that we can eat Christ day by day is a miracle. Day by day, week after week, month after month, and year after year, we eat only one thing—Christ Himself as our heavenly manna.

No Oldness

With the matter of eating, there is no oldness involved. When the children of Israel ate the lamb, they were to let nothing of it remain (Exo. 12:10). When they ate the manna in the wilderness, the same manna was fresh every day. A person could never eat old manna. The children of Israel, however, did not have the faith. They tried to save the manna and went against what Moses told them. The manna that they tried to save "bred worms and stank" (16:20). We cannot store the manna, so we need to eat Christ in a fresh way day by day every morning. Some people buy groceries once a week and store these groceries in their refrigerator, but it is not possible to store manna in this way. Day by day the same heavenly food comes from the heavens in a new and fresh way. We have to keep up to date with the Lord. We always have to eat today's manna.

THE PRODUCE OF THE LAND

Finally, the children of Israel went into the good land to enjoy the produce of the land. The lamb, the manna, and the produce of the land are types of Christ. Christ is our Lamb, our manna, and our land. As the land Christ is rich to the fullest extent. This land is "a land of wheat and barley and vines and fig trees and pomegranates; a land of olive trees with oil and of honey; a land in which you will eat bread without scarcity; you will not lack anything in it" (Deut. 8:8-9). All this produce of the good land is Christ Himself for our enjoyment. Joshua 5:10-12 says, "The children of Israel camped in Gilgal; and they held the Passover on the fourteenth day of the month in the evening on the plains of Jericho. And on the day after the Passover, on that very day, they ate of the produce of the land, unleavened cakes and parched grain. And the manna ceased on that day, when they ate of the produce of the land; and there was no longer manna for the children of Israel, but they ate of the yield of the land of Canaan that year." In this short portion of the Word, Joshua puts these three items together. He mentions the passover lamb, the manna, and the produce of the land. These items are Christ as food to us for life. Thank the Lord for the lamb, the manna, and the land with all its rich produce.

CHAPTER FOUR

ASPECTS OF DRINKING
IN THE OLD TESTAMENT

Scripture Reading: Exo. 15:22-27; 17:1-7; Num. 20:1-13; 21:16-18; 1 Cor. 10:3-4

We saw in the last chapter that the history of the children of Israel was one of eating. In this chapter we want to see that the history of the children of Israel is not only one of eating but also one of drinking. In Genesis 2 are the tree of life for eating and the river of water for drinking. These two items go together to produce the precious materials which are good for God's building. From Genesis 2 onward with the history of God's chosen people, there were always the two matters of eating and drinking. These two matters are seen throughout the entire Bible. With today's chosen people of God, there must also be the matters of eating and drinking because these are the two main aspects of the maintenance of life. For life we need to eat and drink. Eating and drinking enable us to enjoy and maintain life.

THE BITTER WATERS MADE SWEET
BY THE RESURRECTED CHRIST

The history of the children of Israel started with the eating of the passover lamb in Exodus 12. Soon after they had eaten the passover and crossed the Red Sea to come out of Egypt, they became short of water. Exodus 15:22 tells us that "they went three days in the wilderness and found no water." They came to Marah, which means "bitterness," because the waters of Marah were bitter and not good for drinking. It is significant that the journey from the Red Sea to Marah was exactly three days. Their being three days in the wilderness in thirst means that they were buried for three days, that they were in death. The third day may be considered as the day of resurrection since the Lord Jesus was raised on the third day (1 Cor. 15:4). When the children of Israel came to the bitter waters of Marah on the third day, the Lord showed Moses a tree, and when Moses cast this tree into the waters, the waters became sweet (Exo. 15:25). We may say that the tree is the resurrected Christ because this tree was cast into the bitter waters of Marah after the children of Israel had traveled three days in the wilderness.

Because the children of Israel were short of water and came to a place of bitter waters, they began to murmur and complain. This is a good picture of the people of God when they are short of water. If a local church is short of spiritual water, be sure that there will be fighting, chiding, murmuring, and complaining there. If chiding, complaining, and murmuring are present in a local church, that is a proof of dryness, a proof of thirst. If we had no water to drink for three days, no doubt, many of us would be chiding, fighting, and murmuring because of the shortage of water. We need to realize that we have a living tree, the resurrected Christ. If we would put this resurrected Christ into our bitterness, allowing the resurrected Christ to come into our situation, the bitter waters will become the sweet waters.

At Marah, even before the law was given, the Lord made for the children of Israel a statute and an ordinance (v. 25). This signifies that if we have the drinkable, sweet, living water among us, out of this living water there will spontaneously be a living statute and ordinance. The more we drink of the living water, the sweet water of the resurrected Christ, the more we are regulated. The statute and ordinance are not of the law of letters but are the living statute and ordinance of the drinking of the living water.

I believe that the statute made at Marah may have been that there was to be no more chiding or murmuring. After the bitter waters were made sweet, the children of Israel may have said that there was no more need for them to chide or murmur, so they made a statute to this effect. There is no need to chide or murmur when there is plenty of water and when the waters are sweet. If there is much chiding and murmuring in a local church, there will be much sickness in that church. If we murmur all the time, we will be sick. Murmuring opens the door to the enemy to bring in all kinds of diseases. If we are those who murmur, complain, and chide, we are the same as the Egyptians, the worldly people. In most worldly associations or societies, the people murmur, chide, and even fight with one another. Should we have this kind of situation or condition among the people of God in a local church?

Our chiding or murmuring is a kind of disease. We are sick spiritually, and this spiritual sickness can result even in physical sickness. In 1 Corinthians 11 Paul told the Corinthians that many among them were weak and sick, and a number were even dead (v. 30) because of their murmuring, chiding, and divisiveness. The Corinthians were against one another because they were short of the sweet water of the resurrected Christ. If we have the resurrected Christ in our situation, our situation will be so sweet with the living water. Then we will have a statute that we would never chide, murmur, complain, or fight with one another. Our ordinance is to praise the Lord and to shout for joy with no chiding and no murmuring. This ordinance is an issue of the sweet waters. If we are enjoying the resurrected Christ in our situation and the sweetness of the living water, we will not have any kind of disease.

If murmuring and chiding can be found in a local church, this proves that there are Egyptian diseases there. If there is an absence of murmuring and chiding, there is a living statute made of the sweet, living water that instructs us not to criticize, chide, murmur, complain, or fight with one another. This statute was not given at Sinai but was made at Marah where the children of Israel had the sweet waters. Exodus 15:26 says, "If you will listen carefully to the voice of Jehovah your God and do what is right in His eyes and give ear to His commandments and keep all His statutes, I will put none of the diseases on you which I have put on the Egyptians; for I am Jehovah who heals you." We should not have diseases or illness among us, because the Lord is the Healer to us, and

His healing is in the sweet waters. We have the Lord as our Healer.

Following their experience at Marah, the children of Israel came to Elim, where there were twelve springs of water and seventy palm trees (v. 27). The palm tree in the Bible signifies the victory of the evergreen life. We have to praise the Lord for the palm tree, for the victory of life. Seventy is ten times seven. Seven is the number of completion, and ten is the number of fullness, so Elim is a place full of victories of life. There were also twelve springs of water at Elim. Twelve is composed of four times three. The number four signifies the creatures, especially mankind, and the number three signifies the Triune God. Therefore, four times three, the number twelve, is the mingling of divinity with humanity. The springs at Elim are for the mingling of divinity with humanity. God as the living water is flowing into His chosen people to be mingled with them. The resurrection life at Elim flows and grows. It flows out of God into us, and through this flowing, it grows upward to express the riches and victory of the divine life.

We need Christ as the tree, the resurrected One, to be put into our situation. Then we will have the sweet waters. Out of these sweet waters will issue a statute and an ordinance not to murmur or chide but to praise. Our situation should not be one of murmuring, but one of praising. We need an ordinance of saying, "O Lord, Amen, Hallelujah." Our ordinance and our statute is not to chide, criticize, murmur, or complain, but always to praise. This statute and ordinance was not of the letter of the law but of the drinking of the sweet waters. Eventually, we are brought to a situation at Elim with twelve springs of water and seventy palm trees. This situation is full of the flowing of life for the mingling of divinity with humanity and full of the victories of life for praising the Lord. Elim is a place full of praises coming out of life.

DRINKING OF CHRIST
AS THE SPIRITUAL ROCK

In Exodus 15 the children of Israel enjoyed the sweet waters, and in chapter 16 they ate the heavenly manna. In chapter 17 they came to a place where they were short of water again. Whenever they were short of water, there was chiding, murmuring, complaining, and fighting among them (vv. 1-4). They became sick again because they were short of water. At a certain time, the ordinance of praising in a local church may be gone. Instead of praising, there may be murmuring and criticizing. At that time the church will be sick. Today we may have the ordinance of praising, but later we may have the ordinance of criticizing.

Because the children of Israel were short of water, again they began to chide Moses and murmur against him. "So the people thirsted there for water, and the people murmured against Moses and said, For what reason did you bring us up out of Egypt; to kill us and our children and our livestock with thirst? So Moses cried out to Jehovah, saying, What shall I do with this people? A little more, and they will stone me. And Jehovah said to Moses, Pass on before the people, and take with you some of the elders of Israel; and take in your hand your staff with which you struck the River, and go. I will be standing before you there upon the rock in Horeb; and you shall strike the rock, and water will come out of it so that the people may drink. And Moses did so in the sight of the elders of Israel" (vv. 3-6).

It seemed that the Lord was saying to Moses, "Take your staff to do something. I have given you the power, the authority. The staff is in your hand. Didn't you use the staff to do many things in My authority, in My power? Now take the staff and strike the rock." This signifies that Christ as the living rock was smitten by the power of the law. Moses represents the law. Christ on the cross was smitten by the authority, by the power, of the law. Then the living water came out of Christ, the smitten rock. John 19:34 tells us that out of the side of the crucified Christ came forth blood and water. The blood was for redemption, and the water was for life impartation. Christ as the living rock had to be smitten by the power of the law in order for the living water to flow out from Him.

In a sense, as the members of Christ, we all have to be smitten by the power of the law. We have to be dealt with by God's authority. Christ was dealt with by the power of the law, and today as members of Christ we all have to be dealt with by God's authority. Then we will have the living water.

In Exodus 15 is Christ as the tree, and in chapter 17 is Christ as the rock. The tree signifies the resurrected Christ, and the rock signifies the smitten, crucified Christ. If we are going to have the living water, the sweet water, the flowing water, in the local churches, we have to apprehend and experience the crucified and resurrected Christ. The resurrected Christ is the tree to us, and the crucified Christ is the rock to us. First Corinthians 10:4 tells us that the children of Israel all drank the same spiritual drink of the spiritual rock which followed them, which was Christ.

SPEAKING TO THE ROCK
TO DRINK THE LIVING WATER

Numbers 20:1-13 tells us that after a certain time, the children of Israel came back again to Massah and Meribah. This third occasion of the children of Israel's drinking is a repetition of the second one. *Massah* means "test," and *Meribah* means "strife" or "contention." It was at Massah and Meribah that the children of Israel tested and strove with the Lord. By that time the children of Israel were circling in their travels. They were wandering in the wilderness and came back again to the same spot. If they had not wandered but had gone on, they would never have had a repetition of their experience at Massah. Because they were wandering and would not go on, they came back again to the place of tempting the Lord and striving with the Lord. If a local church would not go on but would wander, sooner or later that church will have a repetition of this poor experience.

The children of Israel chided Moses again, and this time they really offended Moses. Moses went to the Lord, and the Lord told Moses to speak to the rock so that the water could flow out of it. There was no need for Moses to strike the rock, because it had already been struck and cleft. But Moses was angry with the people of Israel and called them rebels (v. 10). This incident shows us that we need to be careful regarding how we treat and speak about the Lord's children. Even if they are poor, we should not be so angry. Even if they are poor, it is safe to say that they are very good. If you are wise, you will not go to the parents of a certain boy or girl to say something bad about them. Regardless of how poor or how bad their children are, do not go to their parents to say something bad about them. It is best to tell the parents something good about their children.

The book of Numbers tells us the story of Balak hiring Balaam to curse the children of Israel. At that time the children of Israel were very poor. Balak thought that it was the right time for him to hire Balaam to curse them because of the poor situation among them. All Balaam could do, however, was bless the children of Israel. He said that the Lord saw no iniquity or trouble among the children of Israel (23:21). Balaam's prophecy surprised Balak, so he took Balaam to another place to curse the children of Israel. Perhaps if Balaam would see the children of Israel from another angle, from another direction, he would see their real situation and curse them. Eventually, Balaam said, "How fair are your tents, O Jacob, / Your tabernacles, O Israel!" (24:5). All Balaam could say about the children of Israel was something positive. Do not say that the church in your locality is so poor. If you say this, you will lose something.

Moses lost the entry into the good land due to his mistake in his anger at Meribah. Because he was angry, he did something wrong. The Lord did not tell him to strike the rock again. The Lord told him to go and speak to the rock, which had already been struck. When people get angry, it is always easy for them to do something wrong. When you get angry, you must learn the secret of running away from the situation that makes you angry. Do not say anything or do anything. Just run away from the situation, and keep yourself away until your anger is over. Then you may come back to say something. Even Moses, who was an old, experienced, humble, meek, and patient man, did something wrong in his anger.

It is very hard to pass the test of the local churches. In the local churches the leading brothers are always tested by the saints. They may have done many good things for the saints and to the saints, but the saints may forget these things. They may chide the leading ones, fight against them, and say something poor about them. That may cause the leading brothers to be angry. But we need to be careful and not get angry. Do not call the saints rebels, but always speak well concerning them. If you say that the brothers are good and the sisters are nice, you will gain something. Although Moses did something wrong by striking the rock, the Lord was merciful, and the water still came out of the rock. The fact that the rock gave forth water even under the wrongdoing of Moses proves how merciful the Lord is.

The truth is that Christ was struck and cleft on the cross once for all. There is no need for Him to be struck again. We need to realize the accomplished fact that Christ was struck on the cross two thousand years ago. Instead of striking Him again, we just need to speak to Him. When we speak to Him, He will give us the living water. *Hymns,* #248 is very good in this point:

> 1 Fainting in the desert,
>   Israel's thousands stand
>   At the rock of Kadesh.
>   Hark! the Lord's command,
>   Speak to the Rock,
>   Bid the waters flow,
>   Strike not its bosom
>   Opened long ago,
>   Speak to the Rock,
>   Till the waters flow.
>
> Chorus:
>   Speak to the Rock,
>   Bid the waters flow,
>   Doubt not the Spirit,
>   Given long ago;
>   Take what He waiteth,
>   Freely to bestow,
>   Drink till its fulness
>   All Thy being know.

2 Blessed Rock of Ages,
  Thou art open still;
  Thy blest Holy Spirit
  All our being fill;
  Still Thou dost say,
  Wherefore struggle so?
  Call for the Spirit,
  Whisper soft and low,
  Speak to the Rock
  Bid the waters flow.

3 Oh, for trust more simple,
  Fully to believe;
  Oh, for hearts more childlike,
  Freely to receive;
  E'en as a babe,
  On its mother's breast,
  So on Thy bosom
  Let my spirit rest,
  Filled with Thy life,
  With Thy blessing blest.

The more you sing this hymn, the more you will fall in love with it. Christ has already been crucified and riven for us. We do not need to strike Him, but we need to call on Him, to speak to Him, to bid Him to give us the living water.

DIGGING AWAY THE DIRT
TO ENJOY CHRIST AS THE WELL

The fourth occasion of the children of Israel's drinking is recorded in Numbers 21:16-18. They came to a place called Beer, which means "a well." When the children of Israel came to Beer, they came to a well. This is a type of Christ being a well in us. He is not only the cleft rock but also a well of water. The Lord Jesus tells us in John 4:14 that if we drink of Him, we will have a fountain or a well of water within us. Christ is the rock outside of us, and He is the well within us. As the rock outside of us, He needs to be struck. Regarding Christ as the well within us, we need to be dug. There is no need for Christ to be struck again, but there is the need for us to be dug so that Christ as the well can spring up within our inward being. There is much dirt in our inward being blocking the flowing of Christ. All this dirt needs to be dug away.

Numbers 21:18 says, "The well, which the leaders sank, / Which the nobles of the people dug, / With the scepter, with their staffs." A scepter is a royal rod in the ruler's hand related to authority. Psalm 23 indicates that the staff or staffs are for guidance (v. 4). Thus, scepters are for authority, and staffs are for guidance. We need to be dug under the Lord's authority and according to His guidance.

The leaders and nobles of the people would not normally be the ones to dig the well. The people of the lower class would do the digging. But Numbers 21 tells us that the leaders and nobles of the people of God dug the well at Beer. If we are going to enjoy Christ as the well springing up all the time in the local churches, all the leading ones have to take the lead to dig away the dirt under the Lord's authority and according to His guidance. Then we will have a well springing up with living water all the time in the churches because we have the digging by the leaders and the nobles of the people with the scepter and the staffs.

CALLING ON THE LORD TO DRINK THE LIVING WATER

The fifth occasion concerning the matter of drinking in the Old Testament is the occasion of Samson in Judges 15. The Spirit of the Lord had come upon Samson, enabling him to slay a thousand Philistines with the jawbone of an ass. Afterward, Samson was dying of thirst, so he called on Jehovah (v. 18), and "God broke open the hollow place that is in Lehi, and water came forth from it. And when he drank, his spirit returned and he was revived; therefore he called the name of that place En-hakkore, which is in Lehi to this day" (v. 19). En-hakkore means "the fountain of him who called." When we call on the name of the Lord, we drink the living water, and we are revived. The portions of Scripture that we have covered in this chapter cover five occasions that provide us with a full picture of the matter of drinking in the Old Testament.

CHAPTER FIVE

THE FLOW OF LIFE

(1)

Scripture Reading: Psa. 36:8; 46:4; Joel 3:18; Zech. 14:8; Ezek. 47:1, 2, 12; Isa. 55:1-3

In the last chapter we saw five occasions related to the water for drinking recorded in the Old Testament. In Exodus 15 is the tree put into the bitter waters to make them sweet. In Exodus 17 is the smitten, cleft rock flowing out the water of life for the people to drink. Numbers 20 shows us that now that the rock has been cleft, we need to speak to the rock to enjoy its living water. In Numbers 21 is the well within us, requiring that we dig away all the dirt in our being so that the well has a free way to flow out. In Judges 15 Samson called on Jehovah (v. 18) because he was dying of thirst, so God provided him with water to drink, and he was revived. Calling on the name of the Lord is the way to drink the living water and be revived. These five cases show us that the living water quenches our thirst and solves our problems. These instances constitute the first part of the children of Israel's drinking before the building up of the house of God and the city. In this chapter we want to see the second part of the children of Israel's drinking after the building of the house and the city.

DRINKING THE WATER OF LIFE
AFTER THE BUILDING OF GOD'S HOUSE
AND GOD'S CITY

The verses cited in the Scripture reading show us that the water for drinking is always related to either God's house or

God's city. Psalm 36:8 says, "They are saturated with the fat-
ness of Your house, / And You cause them to drink of the river
of Your pleasures." In this verse God's house is mentioned.
Psalm 46:4 says, "There is a river whose streams gladden the
city of God." In this verse the river is in the city. The river
that makes the city glad has streams like the river in the
garden of Eden that was one river parted into four branches
(Gen. 2:10). These two verses in the Psalms show us that the
river is in the house within the city. Because the house is in
the city, the river in the house is also in the city.

Joel 3:18 tells us that a fountain will go forth from the
house of Jehovah. Zechariah 14:8 tells us that living waters
will go forth from Jerusalem, "half of them toward the eastern sea and half of them toward the western sea." The river
flows, on the one hand, toward the Dead Sea to the east and,
on the other hand, toward the Mediterranean Sea to the
west. In Joel and Zechariah we see again that the river is
related to the house and the city. Ezekiel 47 tells us that
water flows out from under the threshold of the house (v. 1).
Finally, Isaiah 55:1 shows us that there is a call in the preaching of the gospel for everyone who thirsts to come to the
waters.

The Inner Flow of the Divine Life
in the Church

We have to be impressed that the house of God comes out
of the flow of life. Genesis 2 shows us that the materials for
the building up of the bride come out of the flow of the water
of life. The issue, the produce, of the flow of life is precious
materials for the building of God's house. After the house is
built, the water comes out of the house. The one hundred
twenty disciples in Acts 1 were individuals who had drunk of
the Lord Jesus (v. 15). The living water flowed into them, and
by the flow of this living water, they were transformed into
precious materials for God's building. The church was built
up with them as the materials. From that time, the sweet
living water was in the church.

The Lord Jesus as the fountain, the source, the spring, of
living water is in the church, the house of God. Before the

building up of the house, the source, the fountain, was Christ.
After the building up of the house, the source, the fountain,
is still Christ. The only difference is that now Christ as the
fountain, the source, of living water is within the building.
The water is flowing from within the house because the fountain is in the house. The water now flows within and out of
the house of God.

At the beginning of our salvation we had the sense that
something within us was flowing, but after a certain period of
time we had the sense that this flow stopped. It stopped
because we had not entered into the practical church life, the
house of God. At the beginning of our salvation, for a certain
period of time the Lord may grant us the flow of the living
water, but this flow cannot be maintained unless we enter
into the church life. Once we get into the local church, the
house, we have the deep sense that the flow within us, which
had been lost, is now recovered. The inner flow of the divine
life is recovered in the local church.

At the beginning of our salvation there was a flow, and
that flow was for the church. But we may not have realized
this. We may have thought that Christ alone was sufficient.
We had the wonderful Christ flowing within us, and we
thought the flow within us would not stop. But the flow did
stop because we did not enter into the church, the house.
One day, however, the Lord in His mercy brought us into
the practical church life, the house. Those of us who are in the
practical church life can testify that we have the sense of a
deeper, wider, and richer flow. Just as there are two parts to
the history of the children of Israel's drinking in the Old
Testament, there are also two parts with those of us who
are in the practical church life. Part of our history of drinking
was before the church life, and another part is after the
church life. The part before the church life was initial and
temporary.

The Constant Flow of Life
in God's House

When we get into God's house, the flow is constant. In
the New Jerusalem, the holy city and the tabernacle of God

(Rev. 21:2-3), the river of water of life flows constantly (22:1). If the flow within us is occasional and not constant, this means that we are not in the house but in the wilderness. With the five occasions of drinking before the building of the house of God, problems were solved by the drinking of the living water, but that water did not flow constantly. Once the house was built and the city was established, the water began to flow constantly. Our problems come back again because we have only the instant flow and not the constant flow. We need to get into the house to enjoy the constant flow of life.

All of us who are in the practical church life can testify of the difference regarding the inner flow of life before and after we came into the church life. After I received the Lord, I experienced the flow. But shortly after that initial experience, the flow was cut off. This flow would come back occasionally and instantly, but then it would stop again. However, since I came into the church life, I have enjoyed the constant flow.

We need to pay our full attention to these two sections in the history of the Lord's children—the section of the water flowing for drinking before the building of the house with the city and the other section afterwards. In the section before the building, the water flows occasionally and instantly, but in the section after the building, the water flows constantly and eternally. Today we should not be in the wilderness but in the house and in the city. We need to be in the house and in the city to have a constant flow of the living water. We should not be satisfied with the occasional flow in the wilderness, but we all need to experience the constant flow in the house of God and in the city of God.

The Flow of Life out of the House
Watering the Dry Land,
Producing Life, and Healing Death

The water to drink before the building, basically speaking, quenches the thirst. But after the house was built, the water not only quenches the thirst but also waters the dry land, produces life, and heals the death. The water at Marah, Massah, Beer, and Lehi is basically for quenching. But in the city within the house is the flowing river, not only to quench but also to water the dry land, produce life, and heal the death.

Psalm 46:4 tells us that the river gladdens the city. If we do not have the water of life, we will be sad. Joel and Zechariah tell us that the river flows from the house within the city to water the desert and to heal the two seas, the Dead Sea on the east and the Mediterranean Sea on the west. The water flowed out of the house through and out of the city to heal the death.

THE FLOWING OF THE LIVING WATER
OUT OF THE HOUSE OF GOD

The Man of Bronze

In Ezekiel 47 the Lord gives us an exceedingly clear picture of the flowing of the living water out of the house of God. Ezekiel tells us that "He brought me back to the entrance of the house" (v. 1) and that "the man went out to the east with the line in His hand" (v. 3) and measured a thousand cubits. The man referred to here is Christ. This man in chapter 47 is the One mentioned in 40:3: "He brought me there, and there was a man, whose appearance was like the appearance of bronze, with a line of flax and a measuring reed in His hand, standing in the gate."

Daniel 10:5-6 says, "I lifted up my eyes and I looked, and there was a certain man, clothed in linen, whose loins were girded with the fine gold of Uphaz. His body also was like beryl, His face like the appearance of lightning, His eyes like torches of fire, His arms and His feet like the gleam of polished bronze, and the sound of His words like the sound of a multitude." In Daniel the Lord was girded at the loins, whereas in Revelation 1 He is girded at the breasts. He was girded at the loins in Daniel because He was still working, but by the time of Revelation 1, the work is accomplished. His being girded at the breasts there signifies His care for the churches in love. Daniel tells us that His arms and His feet were like the gleam of polished bronze, whereas Revelation 1:15 tells us that "His feet were like shining bronze, as having been fired in a furnace." This shows us that the man in

Ezekiel 40 with the appearance of bronze, who is seen again in chapter 47, is Christ.

Christ is not only a man of gold but also a man of bronze. His being a gold man indicates that He is full of divinity, while His being a bronze man indicates that He is the judging One. Bronze in typology signifies divine judgment (Exo. 27:1-6). Shining or polished bronze means that He has first been judged, tested, and proved to be perfect. He is the polished bronze. He is the One who has been judged and tested and is now qualified to judge and test others. In the book of Ezekiel the Lord Jesus is the judging One, the testing One, so He has the measuring line, the measuring reed.

The Flow of Life
for God's Glory

Ezekiel 47:1 says, "Then He brought me back to the entrance of the house, and there was water flowing out from under the threshold of the house to the east (for the house faced east); and the water flowed down below the south side of the house, on the south of the altar." The entrance of the house is also the exit of the house. The word *threshold* may be translated into "passage." The threshold in this verse is the passage of the house. The entrance of the temple is toward the east, toward the rising of the sun, which means that it is toward the glory (Num. 2:3; Ezek. 43:2). The flowing of the water is toward the glory. Everything concerning the flowing must be for God's glory.

The Preeminence
of the Flow of Life

Also, the water comes from the south, or right side of the house. In the Bible the right side is the highest position, the first place. Thus, the flow of life must have the preeminence, the first place. This tells us that we should never forget, neglect, or miss the flow of living water, the flow of life. We have to check with ourselves all the time: "Do we have the flow within us? Are we in the flow?" If we are in the flow, everything is all right regardless of the situation that we are in. As long as we are in the flow, we are one with the Lord.

We have to pay our full attention to the flow and pay the price to get ourselves into the flow. This flow must be on the right side; it must be in the first place; it must have the preeminence.

A Full Consecration to Enjoy the Flow of Life

The flowing is at the south side of the altar. Everything must be put on the altar for the flow of the living water. We do need a full consecration to enjoy the flow of life. We need to consecrate all that we have and all that we are to the Lord.

Being Measured by the Lord
for the Increase of the Flow of Life

Ezekiel 47:3 says, "When the man went out to the east with the line in His hand, He measured a thousand cubits; and He led me through the water, water that was to the ankles." Measuring means to judge or to test. Anything that is measured by God is judged by Him and is tested by Him. To measure something means to test it, to determine whether it is according to a certain standard. Measuring tells us whether the size or weight is right.

To measure also means to possess. In Revelation 21:15 the holy city is measured by God, which means that God is going to possess it. Whatever God measures is what belongs to Him. When one is going to buy a portion of land, the portion that he measures is the portion that he possesses. How much one measures is how much belongs to him. Thus, to measure means to test, to judge, and eventually to possess.

To measure also means to examine. When ladies go to the drapery store in the Far East to buy drapes, they measure the material. While they are measuring, they examine the material to check for holes or imperfections. Even when people buy a plot of land, they measure it, and this measuring includes their examining it. In conclusion, to measure means to judge, to test, to possess, and to examine.

In the house the water is flowing constantly, but the depth of the water depends upon the measuring. Before the man began to measure in verse 3, verse 2 tells us that the water was running out on the south, or right side. The American

Standard Version tells us in the margin that *was running out* can also be translated into "trickled forth." Thus, after the man began to measure, the flow of water began to increase. After the first measuring, the trickle became a flow to the ankles. At this point the flow is still not so deep because there has not been the adequate measuring. Likewise, the flow may not be so deep within because you have not been adequately measured by the Lord. You have only been measured a little. You may be able to declare, "Hallelujah, I am in the church. I am in the house of God, and I have the flow." You may have the flow, but what kind of flow do you have? What kind of flow are you in? Is your flow a trickle or to the ankles?

All of us need to be measured by the man of bronze. The Lord Jesus as the measuring One, the testing One, the possessing One, needs to come in to measure us. We must allow Him to judge us, to test us, in order to possess us. We may say that we have consecrated everything on the altar, but the Lord wants to measure us. He desires to test and examine us. After His measuring, the water increases.

The man of bronze again measured a thousand cubits, and the water came to the knees (v. 4). The more you are measured, tested, judged, and examined, the more you are possessed by the Lord, and the deeper the flow becomes. The third time of measuring by the man of bronze in Ezekiel 47 brings the level of water to the loins (v. 4), a much deeper flow. We may be in the church and in the flow, but how much have we been tested by the Lord? How much have we been judged by the Lord? How much have we allowed the Lord to take possession of us? The Lord examines us by measuring us. The Lord is going to test us, to possess us, and to examine us. He desires to measure everything concerning us, even the small things. He wants to measure our attitude, the way we spend our money, the way we spend our time, and our conduct.

You may declare, "Hallelujah, I am in the local church!" But you have to pass the test. The test we all have to pass is not man's test but the Lord's test. He is the man of bronze holding the measuring reed. You may feel that you are in the local church and that you have put everything on the altar. In His wisdom the Lord would not measure a full four thousand cubits immediately. He measures gradually in units of one thousand cubits. If He would measure us in a complete way at one time, measuring four thousand cubits, we would not be able to take it. In the same way that a mother feeds her little child a little at a time, the Lord measures us little by little. Each time the Lord measures us, He measures one thousand cubits. One thousand is a complete unit in the Bible. The Lord Jesus would not measure you four thousand cubits immediately, but He has to measure you for a complete unit.

The number four refers to the creation and specifically to man as the head of creation. The fact that the measurement by the man of bronze is in four times of one thousand cubits means that our entire being has to be possessed by the Lord. The Lord does not want to possess merely a part of our being but our entire being. Our consecration must be absolute. Absolute means four thousand cubits of being measured by the Lord so that our entire being is taken over by Him. After the fourth time of measurement, Ezekiel tells us that the water became a river that could not be passed through: "For the water had risen, enough water to swim in, a river that could not be crossed" (47:5). Before the first time of measuring, the water trickled forth. After the first time, it came up to the ankles. After the second time, it came to the knees. After the third time, it came to the loins. Finally, after the fourth time, no one could tell how deep the water was. It had become a river that could not be passed through, enough water to swim in.

Before getting into the flow, a person can walk easily on the dry land. It is very convenient to walk on dry land, but to walk in a place where water is trickling forth is inconvenient. After a downpour, the water that trickles on the thorough-fares makes it somewhat inconvenient to walk. When the water comes up to a person's ankles, it is even more bother-some to walk. When it comes up to the knees, it is even more difficult to walk. When the water comes to the loins, a person can still move but with difficulty. The deeper the flow of the water is and the more we are in this flow, the more inconve-nient it becomes. After being measured by the Lord, you will have the feeling that it is harder to move. The more grace you receive, the more you will be limited and bothered.

When the flow of grace rises to the loins, it is very difficult to move. This is the hardest test. At this time you may wish that you were not in the local church, and you may want to get away. However, you cannot get away because you are encompassed with and surrounded by water. When the water is to the loins, your consecration is seventy-five percent; when it is to the knees, your consecration is fifty percent; and when it is to the ankles, your consecration is twenty-five percent. The time when you are seventy-five percent consecrated is the hardest time. At this time you may have sufficient grace so that it is not easy to lose your temper, and yet you do not have sufficient grace to overcome your temper. This is a real dilemma. The grace is there, yet it is not deep enough. You need to be measured again one thousand cubits. Then the consecration will be one hundred percent. When that time comes, no one knows the depth of the water. When there is enough water to swim in, there is no need for you to move. This is the time for you to rest because the flow of life is sustaining you, supporting you, and even carrying you away. At that time, you will be able to say Hallelujah all day long. At that time there is no longer any human strength, human effort, or human struggle. The flow of life carries you along.

Human beings after the fall always like to move about in complete freedom. They do not like to be restricted in any way. When we were on the dry land, it was easy to move. As the water of life began to increase in our being, it became more restricting and bothersome. We may feel that we have much strength and energy, but something within is binding and limiting us. We may have told the Lord, "Lord, I surrender myself to You." But it is not until the fourth time of measuring that we will be fully surrendered. At that time, there is no possibility of exercising our own effort. The only thing we can do in the water is to swim. We cannot cross over it. After we have been completely measured by the Lord, there is no need of our strength, our effort, or our struggle. At that time we will say, "Lord, I surrender myself to the flow. I commit myself to the flow. I stop all my effort and cease all my struggle. I am resting in the flow and will let the flow carry me along." We all need to ask ourselves how many steps of measuring we have passed. The picture in Ezekiel 47 is better than one thousand words. We need to praise the Lord that we are in His house, yet we need to be measured thoroughly by Him.

CHAPTER SIX

THE FLOW OF LIFE

(2)

Scripture Reading: Ezek. 47:1-12; Isa. 55:1-3

In chapter 5 we saw that we need to be those who experience the constant flow of life in God's house and that we need to be measured by the Lord for the increase of the flow of life. In this chapter we want to see more concerning the flow of life in Ezekiel 47 and Isaiah 55.

THE FLOW OF LIFE
OUT OF THE HOUSE OF GOD

Ezekiel is a book of recovery. The recovery of the building of the house starts from chapter 40, and by the end of chapter 46 the building is complete. In chapter 47 the water is flowing out of the builded house. The entire Old Testament is a picture book that can show us something concerning our situation today. By the picture in Ezekiel 47, we can realize that the flow of the divine water always comes out of the building of God. Today we are in the age of recovery, and the flow of the divine life must be out of God's recovered house.

In most of the religious worship services in Christianity, the ones who attend have the sense or feeling of dryness, not of watering. When I was in Christianity, I heard many teachings, but I had the sense of dryness because there was very little flow of the living water. There was hardly any flow because there was no recovery of the house of God. When one enters into a local church which is in a proper situation, he will have the feeling and the sense of watering. We always have the sense of watering when we get into some of the local churches because of the recovery of the building up of the house of God. Where the house is, there is the flow of the living water.

The flow of the living water is out of the house because the source, the fountain, the spring, of the living water is within the house. This source is the Lord Jesus. He is the fountain, and now He has a place on this earth to locate Himself. He has a place to dwell, to get Himself settled. Those of us who met in the various groups in Christianity can testify that when we were meeting there, we did not have the sense that the Lord had settled Himself there. When I was meeting there, I had the sense that the Lord was outside the door. This is similar to what is depicted in Revelation 3 where the Lord as the Head of the church is standing outside the degraded church, knocking at her door (v. 20). We did not have the sense that the Lord was settled there, so we were not satisfied or settled. However, when I came into the practical church life, I had the sense that the Lord Jesus was there, and I became settled there.

The Lord Jesus is within the house as the source of the living water; out of Him the living water flows. To have the local churches built up is a great thing. We have to pay our full attention to the house of God, and we have to stay in the house. Ezekiel told us that the Lord brought him to the entrance of the house (47:1). We need to be impressed with our need for the house. There is much work in today's Christianity, but where is the flow? There is much gospel preaching, Bible teaching, and mission work, but where is the flow? There is the feeling of dryness and not the feeling of watering. Many seeking Christians are dissatisfied due to the dryness. They are seeking after the watering. The seekers of the Lord desire the flow of the living water. Out of the marvelous building of God comes the flow of the living water.

THE LORD'S DESIRE FOR A RIVER

In order for the flow of life to increase within us, within the house, the Lord as the man of bronze has to measure us. He is the testing One, the judging One, the examining One, and the possessing One because He measures us. The more

He measures us, the deeper and the broader the flow will be. After He has measured us fully, the flow will become a river. In every city we need a river. The river comes out of the measuring of the bronze man within the house. To be in the local church alone is not adequate. We all need to be measured by the Lord. We may be in a local church, yet the living water may not be so deep. The flow in the church may not yet be a river. When we are adequately measured by the Lord, we will have the river. The Lord is not content with only a flow of the living water. He desires a river, because the river waters, heals, and produces. In 47:6 the Lord asked Ezekiel, "Son of man, have you seen this?" We all have to see this marvelous picture in Ezekiel.

THE RIVER WATERING THE DESERT
AND HEALING THE DEAD SEA
FOR PRODUCING LIFE

The Lord told Ezekiel in 47:8, "This water flows out toward the eastern region and goes down into the Arabah and goes to the sea; when it flows into the sea, the water of the sea is healed." The river in verse 8 goes down into the Arabah. The Hebrew word *Arabah* means the wilderness, the dry land, the parched land that grows nothing; hence, the desert. This land needs the watering. The river is for watering the dry land and healing the Dead Sea. The Arabah is close to the Dead Sea. Joshua 3:16 refers to the Dead Sea as the sea of the Arabah. The Dead Sea, or the Salt Sea, is near the Arabah. Because of the flow of the river into the sea, the salt water in the sea is healed. The sea now becomes fresh water because the salt has been swallowed up. The river comes first to water the dry land that grows nothing and to heal the death waters. This watering and healing is for the purpose of producing life.

The two basic categories of life produced in Ezekiel 47 are the plant life and the animal life. Verse 7 tells us that "there were very many trees on the bank of the river, on one side and on the other." Trees are of the plant life. The river of water brings forth an abundance of fish (v. 9). Verse 10 says, "Fishermen will stand beside the sea from En-gedi even to

En-eglaim; it will be a place for the spreading of nets. Their fish shall be according to their kinds, like the fish of the Great Sea, very many." According to the Hebrew, *En-gedi* means "the fountain of the kid," and *En-eglaim* means "the fountain of the two calves." Thus, the flow of the river produces trees, fish, and cattle. The fishermen spread their nets on the land from En-gedi to En-eglaim. They spread their nets on the land between these two fountains. The trees, the fish, and the cattle in Ezekiel 47 are mentioned according to the order in Genesis 1. In Genesis 1 the plant life is first, the fish are second, and the cattle are third.

We need En-gedi, and we need En-eglaim, the fountains of the kids and the calves. We must realize that the potential with the Lord's recovery is with the young people. I am happy to see so many "kids" and "calves" in the church life. I am an older saint, and I am also very thankful for all the older saints among us. All the "kids" need the care of the older saints. Although I love and appreciate all the older saints, deep within me I realize that the future, the prosperity, and the potential of the Lord's move is with the young ones, with the kids and with the calves. The many young people among us who are full of life are evidence that the local church is the fountain of the kids and the fountain of the calves.

All of us older saints should be so happy that we have so many kids. The kids are an indication of the freshness in the Lord's recovery. How much we have to thank the Lord for so many young ones among us. We need to thank the Lord that Arabah, the desert, the dry land, the parched wilderness, has become the fountain of kids and of calves. We also need to praise the Lord that the Dead Sea, the Salt Sea, has become the living and fresh sea to produce a multitude of fish. By the flowing of the river, there are also fishermen (Ezek. 47:10). Fishing signifies increase in numbers. All the kids and the calves should be the fishermen. The picture in Ezekiel 47 shows us that along with the river are the trees, the fish, the kids, the calves, the fishermen, and their nets.

OUR NEED TO BE MEASURED
FOR THE LORD'S MOVE

The main point for us in Ezekiel 47 is that we all need to be willing to be measured. There is no need for us to struggle, to strive, or to exercise our effort to do anything. The only need is that we have to be willing to be measured again and again and again and again. We need to tell the Lord, "Lord, I am willing to be measured." Then the flow will eventually become the river. If the saints in a local church are willing to be measured again and again and again and again, four times to one hundred percent, there will be a river to water the parched desert, to heal the dead sea, to grow the trees and produce the fish, and to produce the kids and the calves. What we need is to be measured for the Lord's move. We need to be tested, examined, taken over, and possessed by the Lord.

When the water is to the ankles, that means that only a small part of our being is possessed by the Lord. When the water is risen to the loins, part of our being is possessed by the Lord, but another part is still free. If we are willing to be measured up to one hundred percent, we will be fully swallowed up by the living water. Then in one sense, we lose all our freedom, but in another sense we are really free. When we are fully possessed by the Lord, we will be fully freed. The flow of the living water will carry us on forward toward the goal. If we are willing to be built up as the house of the Lord, we will have the Lord within us as the source of the living water. If we are willing to be measured in order to be possessed again and again by the Lord until eventually we are possessed to the uttermost, we will have enough water to swim in, a river that cannot be crossed.

The flowing river waters the dry land, heals the dead sea, produces the trees, brings in the fish, and brings in the kids and the calves. Because of the river there are the farming with all the trees, the fishing to bring in the fish, and the ranching to take care of the kids and the calves. If we are willing to be built up and measured again and again, we will have the trees, the fish, and the cattle. This means that we will have the food, which includes the produce of the trees, the produce of the seas, and the produce of the ranch. When the Lord fed the five thousand, He fed them with something of the land, five loaves, and with something of the sea, two fish. The flow of the river issues in the riches of the land and of the sea, the riches of the animal life and the plant life, the riches of Christ.

COMING TO THE WATERS WITHOUT MONEY TO BUY AND EAT

Isaiah 55:1 says, "Ho! Everyone who thirsts, come to the waters, / And you who have no money; / Come, buy and eat." There is no mention of drinking in this verse. It tells us to come to the waters and eat, not drink. Furthermore, this verse tells the one who has no money to come and buy. How can we come to the waters to eat and come to buy without money?

Ezekiel 47 tells us that there were many trees on the banks of the river (v. 12), showing us that when we come to the waters, we come to the food. Our intention may be merely to drink, but eventually we also get something to eat. The drinking and the eating go together. In Genesis 2 is the tree of life with a river flowing out of Eden to water the garden (vv. 9-10). At the end of the Bible is the river of water of life with the tree of life growing, spreading, and proceeding along its two sides (Rev. 22:1-2). When we come to the waters, there is food for us to eat.

Now we must see how the Lord can tell us to come and buy without money and without price. In Revelation 3 the Lord counseled the church in Laodicea to buy from Him although they were wretched, miserable, poor, blind, and naked (vv. 17-18). On the one hand, we do not have the money to buy, but on the other hand, we cannot say that we have nothing. We may not have money, but we have ourselves. We have to pay ourselves as the cost. We have to give ourselves to the Lord. Isaiah 55:3 says, "Incline your ear and come to Me." This is the price. The price is not the money. The price is not what we have. The price is what we are. We have to pay ourselves as the price to the Lord.

Whenever we come to the waters, the food is there, and whenever we feel that we have nothing, we have ourselves.

The Lord wants us. Thus, He calls us to come and give ourselves to Him. The price to buy the gold in the epistle to Laodicea is to open the door (Rev. 3:20). To open the door is to give ourself to the Lord. We all need to tell the Lord, "Lord, I give myself to You." If we are thirsty, we need to come and buy without money but with ourselves. We need to come and give ourselves to the Lord. When we pay this price, we are free to drink. Also, when we come to drink, we get the food because the water includes the tree of life.

THE SURE MERCIES SHOWN TO DAVID

The last part of Isaiah 55:3 says, "I will make an eternal covenant with you, / Even the sure mercies shown to David." Just as the statute and ordinance were made with the drinking in Exodus 15, an eternal covenant is made here with the call to the thirsty ones to come to the waters and eat. As we are drinking and eating, an eternal covenant is made. This covenant is a contract or an agreement signed by the Lord to us. The Lord becomes bound to us. When we give ourselves to the Lord for the drinking and get the food, the Lord makes an eternal covenant with us, which means that we have a secured, constant enjoyment. Our enjoyment of the Lord becomes constant, secured, and insured. This eternal covenant is the best insurance company to insure our enjoyment of the sure mercies shown to David. The sure mercies shown to David are all that the Lord is for the house of David. All that the Lord is as mercies to the house of David is our secured portion by an eternal covenant.

We can realize by our fellowship thus far that the divine life is always involved with the matters of drinking and eating. If we do not drink and eat, life is lost. The divine life is in the tree and in the river, and we receive this life by drinking and eating. Whenever we come to the waters, we receive not only the waters but also the food. When we eat and drink the Lord, He makes an eternal covenant with us. This covenant is the Lord's signed agreement or insurance policy whereby all the mercies shown to David become sure to us. The sure mercies are secured, insured, and guaranteed by His eternal covenant. All that the Lord is today is the sure mercies to the house of David. Today we are the house of David enjoying the sure mercies shown to David, which are the riches of the divine life.

CHAPTER SEVEN

LIFE VERSUS KNOWLEDGE

Scripture Reading: John 1:1-4, 29; 3:36; 5:21, 39-40; 10:10b;
11:25a; 14:6a; Col. 3:4a; Heb. 7:16; Acts 5:20; 1 Pet. 1:23;
1 Cor. 4:15; 8:1; 2 Tim. 4:3; 2 Cor. 3:6

In the previous chapters we have seen the matter of life
in the Old Testament with the tree as the food and the river
as the drink. Eventually, we saw that the food and the drink
are one. When we are thirsty and come to the waters, we get
the food. The matters of eating and drinking span the entire
Old Testament. The verses we have covered on eating and
drinking start in Genesis 1—2 and end in Zechariah 14. In
this chapter we want to turn our attention to the matter of
life in the New Testament and see how life is versus knowledge. To see the central matter of life in the Bible, we must
get into the concept and the spirit of the Bible.

CREATION, LIFE, AND REDEMPTION
IN GENESIS 1—3 AND JOHN 1

Genesis tells us that in the beginning God created, and
then He presented Himself as life to man. Because man fell,
God had to redeem fallen man in order that life might still be
made available to him. Genesis 3:21 tells us that God made
coats of skin of the sacrifice for Adam and Eve and clothed
them. In order to make coats of the skin of the lambs, God
probably killed the lambs in the presence of Adam and Eve.
Thus, the blood of the lambs was shed, for without shedding
of blood there is no forgiveness (Heb. 9:22). Adam experienced
the anticipated redemption of God.

The first chapter of John's Gospel in the New Testament
has the same spiritual points and concept as the first three

chapters of Genesis in the Old Testament. John 1 tells us that in the beginning was the Word and the Word was God (v. 1). Creation came into being through God as the Word, and in Him was the life presented to man (vv. 3-4). Because of the problem of the fall of the human race, there is the need of redemption. Thus, John 1:29 says, "Behold, the Lamb of God, who takes away the sin of the world!" We should not think that the New Testament has a different thought or concept from the Old Testament. The Old and New Testaments are one book. The Old Testament is a book of pictures, while the New Testament gives us the definition of these pictures. The thought, the concept, and the spirit of the Old and New Testaments are exactly the same.

LIFE IN THE GOSPEL OF JOHN

Nearly every chapter of the Gospel of John tells us something about life. In the Scripture reading of this chapter we have selected some important verses concerning life. John 3:36 says, "He who believes into the Son has eternal life; but he who disobeys the Son shall not see life, but the wrath of God abides upon him." According to John 1, the Son in whom we believe is the One in the beginning, the Word, God, the Creator, the One with life in Him, and the Lamb who takes away our sin. We have to believe in this One so that we may have life. If we do not believe in this One, we cannot have life or see life.

John 5:21 says, "Just as the Father raises the dead and gives them life, so also the Son gives life to whom He wills." The Son's intention is to give life, and His coming is to give life. We have to remember the phrase *the Son gives life*. Thus, the Lord says in John 10:10b, "I have come that they may have life and may have it abundantly." In John 11:25a the Lord told Martha, "I am the resurrection and the life." In John 14:6 He declared that He was the life. These verses show that Christ Himself is the tree of life. Following man's redemption, the tree of life is again presented to man in the New Testament. Colossians 3:4a tells us that Christ is our life.

LIFE VERSUS THE LAW

In the New Testament we can see not only the reality of

the tree of life but also the reality of the tree of knowledge. Just as in the Old Testament, we can see the tree of knowledge next to the tree of life in the New Testament. Hebrews 7:16 tells us that Christ has been constituted the High Priest "not according to the law of a fleshy commandment but according to the power of an indestructible life." In this verse there are two sources: the law and the life. The law is on the side of the tree of knowledge, and the life is on the side of the tree of life. In this verse are the two trees, the tree of knowledge alongside the tree of life. Genesis 2:9 indicates that these two trees are very close to one another. They are not far away from one another, but they are standing alongside one another. If we are careless, we may touch the tree of knowledge instead of the tree of life; we may think that we are touching the tree of life because the tree of knowledge is so close to the tree of life.

The law is good (Rom. 7:12, 16), and anything that is good is very close to life. Everything related to life is good. With the indestructible and endless life, nothing is bad and everything is good. The commandments of the law are also good, so they are very close to life. According to our fallen, natural mentality and discernment, we think that anything good is life. But our minds need to be renewed and transformed to realize that something good may not be life. To consider anything good as life is absolutely wrong. This is a concept of the fallen mentality. In Hebrews 7:16 the law is related to the tree of knowledge, and the life is related to the tree of life.

THE WORDS OF LIFE

In Acts 5:20 the angel charged Peter and the apostles, "Go and stand in the temple and speak to the people all the words of this life." Peter and the apostles were not charged to go and speak merely the word. They were charged to speak the words of this life. The law is close to life, and the word is even closer. Many may claim that they are preaching and teaching the word, but are they speaking the words of this life? In this verse *words* is not the Greek word *logos* but *rhema*. *Logos* is the constant word, and *rhema* is the instant word. The constant word could be the tree of knowledge, but the instant words that the Lord speaks are spirit and life (John 6:63). Because the tree of knowledge and the tree of life are so close to one another, one could take the tree of knowledge and think that he is taking the tree of life. It is hard to discern life from knowledge because life and knowledge are so close to one another.

THE LIVING WORD OF GOD

First Peter 1:23 says, "Having been regenerated not of corruptible seed but of incorruptible, through the living and abiding word of God." A seed is a container of life. The word of God is the incorruptible seed that contains God's life. Through this word, this seed, we have been regenerated. Peter used the adjective *living* to describe the word of God. *Word* here in Greek is *logos,* but Peter pointed out that we were regenerated through the living *logos.* We may have the word and not have the living word. When I was a child, I received the word in Sunday school. Although I went to Sunday school, I was never regenerated or born again there. One day, however, I received the living word, and at that time I was born again. The word by itself is the tree of knowledge, but the living word is the tree of life.

GUIDES VERSUS FATHERS

First Corinthians 4:15 says, "Though you have ten thousand guides in Christ, yet you do not have many fathers; for in Christ Jesus I have begotten you through the gospel." Guides, teachers, or instructors are good, but these guides are related to the tree of knowledge. The guides are a matter of knowledge, but the fathers are a matter of life. Fathers impart life to their children whom they beget, and the apostle was such a father who imparted the divine life into the Corinthians so that they became children of God and members of Christ. Again, we can see how hard it is to discern life from knowledge.

KNOWLEDGE VERSUS LOVE

In 1 Corinthians 8:1 Paul tells us, "Knowledge puffs up, but love builds up." The outward, objective knowledge that puffs up comes from the tree of the knowledge of good and evil, the source of death. The spiritual (not fleshly) love, which is an expression of life as described in 1 Corinthians 13, builds up. It comes from the tree of life, the source of life. Knowledge is something of the tree of knowledge, and love is of the tree of life.

HEALTHY TEACHING

Second Timothy 4:3 says, "The time will come when they will not tolerate the healthy teaching; but according to their own lusts they will heap up to themselves teachers, having itching ears." Teaching is something of knowledge, but *healthy* implies the matter of life. Anything that is healthy refers to the health of life. What we need is not merely the teaching but the healthy teaching. A person's teaching might be quite sound but still dead. We need the healthy teaching, the teaching with life.

Second Timothy 4:3 tells us that the ones who will not tolerate the healthy teaching "according to their own lusts...heap up to themselves teachers, having itching ears." These ones cannot bear with the healthy teaching, but they heap up teachers because they have itching ears, ears that seek pleasing speaking for their own pleasure.

In 1964 I was invited to San Diego, and the responsible one in this certain Christian group put up a sign that told people to hear Witness Lee. When I saw this sign, I told the one responsible to take it down; otherwise, I would not be able to speak. Some Christians attend conference after conference, and there is no change in their life. These ones are addicted to listening to good speakers. They have itching ears, and these good speakers become a drug to them. Many teachings have been heard, but their daily life remains the same. They have only heaped up to themselves teachers who tickle their itching ears.

THE LETTER VERSUS THE SPIRIT

Second Corinthians 3:6 tells us that the apostles were "ministers of a new covenant, ministers not of the letter but of the Spirit; for the letter kills, but the Spirit gives life."

Genesis 2 shows us that the tree of knowledge is a tree of death. God warned Adam that if he ate of the tree of knowledge, he would surely die (v. 17). The New Testament says that the letter kills. When Paul talked about the letter, he was not referring to the letter of a newspaper but to the letter of the Bible. In a sense, the Bible kills. In 2 Corinthians 3:6 the letter is versus the Spirit.

THE SCRIPTURES AND
THE LORD HIMSELF

The Lord Jesus told the Jewish religionists, "You search the Scriptures, because you think that in them you have eternal life; and it is these that testify concerning Me. Yet you are not willing to come to Me that you may have life" (John 5:39-40). Since the Scriptures testify concerning the Lord, they should not be separated from the Lord. We may contact the Scriptures and yet not contact the Lord. Only the Lord can give life. If we have the Scriptures without the Lord, we cannot receive life. Without Christ, even the Scriptures are merely knowledge. Instead of finding life in the Bible, we could get killed by the Bible. Without Christ, the Bible is a book of the letter, and the letter kills.

THE NEED TO DISCERN THE DIFFERENCE
BETWEEN KNOWLEDGE AND LIFE

The verses we have looked at thus far show us that knowledge is very close to life. Satan is so subtle. He causes people to focus on items such as law, work, word, guides, knowledge, teaching, and the letter of the Bible. There is nothing bad about these items. Some may ask, "What is wrong with the law, the divine *logos,* guides, knowledge, teaching, and the letter of the Bible?" May the Lord be merciful to us that we may discern the difference between knowledge and life. The tree of knowledge is not only related to evil but also to good. It is the tree of the knowledge of *good* and evil. I believe that the tree of life and the tree of knowledge were very much the same in appearance (Gen. 2:9; cf. 3:6). In his subtlety Satan always turns us to the tree of knowledge and away from the tree of life. The Bible says that we were regenerated through the

living word, but we may not see the word *living*. The Bible
says that we need fathers, but we may be looking for guides or
instructors. The Bible uses the term *healthy teaching*, but we
may drop the word *healthy* when we talk about teaching.

We need to see the difference between knowledge and life
in the verses we have pointed out. We must see the contrast
between law and life, between the constant word and the
instant words of life, between the *logos* and the living *logos*,
between the guides and the fathers, between knowledge and
life, between teaching and healthy teaching, between letter
and Spirit, and between the Scriptures in themselves and the
living Lord. All the verses we have discussed show us that
the tree of knowledge is still with us today. The local church is
something of life, but the teaching concerning the local
church may only be knowledge. We want the local churches
but not the mere doctrinal teaching concerning the local
churches. If we only take the teaching regarding certain
items, this teaching becomes the knowledge that kills.

We need to be impressed that in both the Old and New
Testaments, there are the tree of life and the tree of knowledge, and these two trees are still with us today. We need to
pray, "O Lord, be merciful to me. I do not want to care for
knowledge, because knowledge brings in death. Keep me
focused on the tree of life." Many times we may have been
deceived unconsciously. The subtle one, Satan, may creep in to
distract us from the tree of life with the best knowledge.
Regardless of how good the knowledge is, it is still the knowledge that kills.

We need to thank and praise the Lord that He is life to us.
We should not care for what is good or evil, right or wrong,
according to the tree of knowledge, but we need to focus our
entire being on the flow of life. What good is it to be right in
our doctrine and be dead? May the Lord open our eyes to see
what He is after today. Today the Lord desires a group of
people to enjoy Him as life. He presented Himself as life that
we might have life and might have it more abundantly. By
His mercy, our eyes need to be opened to see what kind of
damage the tree of knowledge has brought in. We should not
care for knowledge but for life.

In the beginning was the Word, who was God. In Him was life, and He became the Lamb of God to take away our sins. The Lamb became the life-giving Spirit (1 Cor. 15:45b) to impart Himself as life into our being. Day by day and moment by moment, we need to contact Him. When we contact the Bible, we need to contact Him not merely by exercising our mind but by exercising our spirit. When we exercise our spirit to touch the Word, we touch the tree of life. The tree of life and the tree of knowledge are still with us today. These two trees are very close to one another. We have to be aware so that we take in only life and not the deadening knowledge. We have to be on the alert so that we will not be deceived.

CHAPTER EIGHT

EATING AND DRINKING
IN THE NEW TESTAMENT

Scripture Reading: John 4:14; 6:35, 57, 63; 7:37-39; 1 Cor. 3:2; 10:3-4; Heb. 5:12b-14a; 1 Pet. 2:2-3; Rev. 2:7b; 3:20; 7:16-17; 21:6b; 22:1-2, 17; Matt. 22:2-3; Luke 14:16-17; 15:22-23; 1 Cor. 10:21; Rev. 19:9

EATING AND DRINKING—
THE CENTRAL THOUGHT IN GOD'S ECONOMY

Eating and drinking Christ is the central thought in God's economy. This central thought of eating and drinking is not only in the Old Testament but also in the New Testament. The concept of eating and drinking starts at the very beginning of the Bible in Genesis and continues until the end of the Bible in Revelation. In God's economy God does not present Himself to us as a kind of religion, but He presents Himself to us as food and drink. If we realize the proper significance of the verses in the Scripture reading, we will see that eating and drinking is the central thought in the New Testament.

The Gospel Being a Feast

In Matthew 22 the Lord Jesus likened the gospel of God to a marriage or wedding feast, a great supper, prepared by a king for his son (vv. 1-14). Thus, the gospel is a matter of enjoyment by eating and drinking.

In Luke 14:16-17 the Lord Jesus again likens the gospel to a great dinner. God, as the certain man, sent His slave to tell those who had been invited, "Come, for all things are now ready" (v. 17). God has prepared His full salvation as a great dinner. We come not to learn teachings but to enjoy by eating and drinking. When we were saved, we started the enjoyment of eating. After we are saved, the Lord always sets a feast before us.

When I was saved, although no one told me, I did have the sense that something within me was just for my enjoyment. It was so nourishing, so refreshing, so watering. I was so happy in spirit. But soon after my initial experience, I was turned to care only for teachings. I became filled with teachings, but within I was empty. Christianity is a religion full of teachings, but the Lord's desire is to recover His gospel as a real feast. The gospel is a feast where all things are ready, and we simply come to eat, drink, and enjoy.

The central concept of the New Testament is eating and drinking Christ in order that we may feast on Christ. In Luke 15, when the prodigal son returned, the father told his slaves to put the best robe on him, a ring on his hand, and sandals on his feet (v. 22). For his body there was the robe, for his hand the ring, and for his feet the sandals. These items signify the Father's outward justification through Christ. This outward clothing, however, was not sufficient to meet the son's need since he was starving. He needed food within him. His father first adorned him to make him worthy, thus qualifying him to enter the father's house and feast with the father. After the outward adornment, the father told his slaves, "Bring the fattened calf; slaughter it, and let us eat and be merry" (v. 23).

We need not only the outward adorning but also the inward filling. The robe, the ring, and the sandals are the outward side, the side of justification by the blood of Christ. In the observance of the passover, the blood covered the house (Exo. 12:7). Under the covering of the blood, the people enjoyed the meat of the lamb (v. 8). Likewise, under the covering of the robe, the prodigal son enjoyed the slaughtered, fattened calf with his father. This is the inward side, which signifies the inward enjoyment of Christ as our life supply. Christ is the robe, and Christ is also the fattened calf. Christ is for our outward covering, and Christ is also for our inward filling. We should enjoy Him as the fattened calf day by day. In the Father's house we have a feast, a table.

Before the prodigal son came back, he prepared himself to be treated as a slave, laboring day by day for his father (Luke 15:19). But his father did not want his son to labor for him but to feast with him. When we come to the local church, we must drop the thought of coming to labor. We come to the Father's house, the local church, for feasting. In the Father's house there is a table waiting for us to come and feast. Just come to eat and be merry (v. 23). The Lord Jesus will be satisfied, the Father will be happy, and we will be filled. We all need such a feast.

The Lord's Table
Being a Weekly Feast

The Lord's table is also a feast to us. Week by week as we come to the Lord's table, we have a feast. In the past when I attended the so-called communion service, I was never told that the Lord's supper was a table, a feast. I was taught to take the holy communion by first examining myself to see whether I was sinful or not. I would ask myself about my heart, my mind, my thinking. I would ask how I was with my parents, teachers, schoolmates, neighbors, or friends. I was then taught to remember the Lord by remembering how He was God, how He became a man, how He was born in a manger, and so forth. However, I was not told that at the Lord's table I have to enjoy Him; that is, I have to eat Him and to drink Him. To examine ourselves and to remember what the Lord did for us is certainly not wrong. However, the divine concept is that to remember the Lord is simply to eat and drink Him, to enjoy Him.

First Corinthians 11:24-25 says, "This is My body, which is given for you; this do unto the remembrance of Me...This cup...drink it, unto the remembrance of Me." The real remembrance of the Lord is to eat the bread and drink the cup (v. 26), that is, to participate in, to enjoy, the Lord, who has given Himself to us through His redeeming death. To eat the bread and drink the cup is to take in the redeeming Lord as our portion, as our life and blessing. This is to remember Him in a genuine way. Thus, we remember the Lord not by thinking about Him but by eating, drinking, and enjoying

Him. The Lord's table is a weekly proclamation, a declaration to the whole universe, that we daily enjoy Christ as our food and drink. He is our feast, our enjoyment.

The Marriage Dinner
of the Lamb

Eventually, when He comes, the overcoming believers will join Him to feast at the marriage dinner of the Lamb (Rev. 19:7, 9). That unique, universal wedding feast will last one thousand years. This feast of one thousand years will be a wedding day to Christ because to the Lord a thousand years are like one day (2 Pet. 3:8). During those one thousand years, the church is the bride, and after the one thousand years, the church is the wife (Rev. 21:9-10). The difference between a bride and a wife is that the bride is only the bride on the wedding day. After the wedding day, the bride becomes the wife. On the wedding day there is the bridegroom and the bride; on the following day there is the husband and the wife. The millennial kingdom of one thousand years will be a wedding day to Christ, in which the overcoming believers will be with Christ, enjoying His wedding feast.

An Eternal Feast

The gospel is a feast that will last for eternity; therefore, the Lord's table will never end. The Lord's table today is a foretaste of the coming full taste in eternity. Eventually, that full taste will replace our present foretaste. On the table of this feast, we enjoy Christ Himself, who is for our eating and drinking. We are eating Christ (John 6:35, 57) and drinking the Spirit (7:37-39; 1 Cor. 12:13), who is also Christ Himself (15:45; 2 Cor. 3:17).

EATING AND DRINKING
IN THE GOSPEL OF JOHN

The eating and drinking of Christ is also revealed in the Gospel of John. Throughout the Gospel of John, the Lord Jesus speaks of Himself as life to us (10:10; 4:14; 6:35; 7:38; 14:6). In the first chapter of the Gospel of John, a book showing how the Lord Jesus as life can meet the need of every man, there are five major items: God, the Word, the flesh, the Lamb, and life. In the beginning was the Word, and the Word was God (1:1). This Word, who was God Himself, became flesh (v. 14), which means that He became a man. As a man He is the Lamb of God (v. 29), our Redeemer, and He is also our life (v. 4; 10:10). The Gospel of John begins with God, the Word, the flesh, the Lamb, and life.

In chapter 2 of the Gospel of John, there is a wonderful event—a wedding feast (vv. 1-11). When I was young, I studied this portion of the Word. I understood chapter 1 but not chapter 2. I did not know the meaning of the wedding and of the water being changed to wine. Now I realize much more. At this wedding feast the wine ran out, so the Lord Jesus asked the servants to fill up six stone waterpots with water. These waterpots were for the Jewish rite of purification with water, which signifies religion's attempt to make people clean by certain dead practices. But the Lord changed the water in the waterpots, which were for purification, into wine. This wine was not good for outward cleansing, but for drinking. We must forget about how dirty we are outwardly and drink the Lord as our wine inwardly. Regardless of how much we may be cleansed and purified outwardly, we can still be dead inwardly. The Lord Jesus did not come to merely cleanse us outwardly, but He came for us to drink of Him. He turned the water into wine, changing the cleansing element into the drinking element.

The Lord's life is a feast, not for purification, for outward cleansing, but for inward drinking. The inward drinking will take care of the cleansing. Whatever we drink into us will cleanse us, not from without but from within. This is a kind of metabolic cleansing—a cleansing of life. This is not a cleansing in an outward way but a metabolic cleansing from within by life.

Today I appreciate John 2 to the uttermost. In many places, when I was asked to preach the gospel, I used John 2. I have told people, "You are just the six waterpots because you are a man made on the sixth day (Gen. 1:26, 31); therefore, the number six represents man. Your need is the wine. Your need is life. Do not try to improve yourself, correct yourself, or better yourself. To do so is just to try to cleanse or purify yourself. Your need is not cleansing water but wine to drink." John 2 shows us that our need is not outward cleansing but inward drinking. The concept of John 2 is the eating and drinking of the Lord.

In chapter 3 Nicodemus, a highly educated teacher and an experienced, older man, came to the Lord Jesus and said to Him, "Rabbi, we know that You have come from God as a teacher" (v. 2). The human concept is that we need a teacher and more teaching. The Lord Jesus is so wise. He did not argue with Nicodemus or rebuke him, nor did He speak too much with him. After listening to him, the Lord Jesus answered, "Truly, truly, I say to you, unless one is born anew, he cannot see the kingdom of God" (v. 3). This word really puzzled Nicodemus. He may have thought, "I came to be taught by You, to seek teaching. I recognize You as a rabbi, a teacher, yet I do not understand what You mean by being born anew. An old man such as I cannot go back to my mother's womb and come out again. What kind of teaching is this?"

The Lord Jesus indicated to Nicodemus that to be born anew was not to go back to his mother's womb and come out again. To be born anew is to be born of water and the Spirit (v. 5). That which is born of the flesh is flesh (v. 6). Even if Nicodemus could go back to his mother's womb and come out again, he would still be the same Nicodemus, the same flesh. He needed to be something else. He had to be born of the Spirit. "That which is born of the Spirit is spirit" (v. 6). The Lord's word really puzzled Nicodemus. If you or I were there, we too may have been puzzled along with Nicodemus by the Lord's heavenly language.

The Lord Jesus continued to tell Nicodemus that as Moses lifted up the serpent of bronze in the wilderness, He as the Son of Man must be lifted up (v. 14). All the dying people, bitten by the fiery serpents, had to look at the bronze serpent that Moses lifted up. Whoever looked at the bronze serpent lived (Num. 21:7-9). The Lord was there for Nicodemus to look at Him. Nicodemus had to believe in Him; then he would have eternal life. Nicodemus did not need teaching. His need was eternal life, the life which Christ could give him.

While John 3 is about a highly cultured, very religious, God-seeking, God-fearing, moral person, chapter 4 is about an immoral woman. Although she was quite evil, having had five husbands and living with a sixth who was not her husband, she still tried to speak about religion. She pretended to be religious because the Lord Jesus exposed her evil history. The Lord said to her, "Go, call your husband and come here" (v. 16). She said that she did not have a husband. This was a truth but a lie. She told the Lord Jesus a lie by speaking the truth. The Lord Jesus, responding to her, said, "You have well said, I do not have a husband, for you have had five husbands, and the one you now have is not your husband; this you have said truly" (vv. 17-18). Immediately, she changed the subject from her husbands to the worship of God (vv. 19-20). To talk about her husbands was unpleasant. Because the Lord's word about her husbands touched her conscience, she changed the conversation to the matter of worship.

The Lord Jesus, in His wisdom, also began to speak about the worship of God, saying, "God is Spirit, and those who worship Him must worship in spirit and truthfulness" (v. 24). Eventually, the Lord revealed to her that this Spirit, who is God Himself, and who is the One we must worship, is the very living water (vv. 24, 14). The very God who is Spirit is the water of life. We take the water of life by exercising our spirit to contact Him, that is, to worship Him.

In chapter 3 of the Gospel of John, we are told that we have to be born anew, that is, to have a second birth. Then in chapter 4 the Lord Jesus speaks about drinking (v. 14), in chapter 6 about eating (v. 57), and in chapter 7 about drinking again (vv. 37-38). Drinking and eating seem to be two separate things, yet actually they are one. John 6:35 says, "I am the bread of life; he who comes to Me shall by no means hunger, and he who believes into Me shall by no means ever thirst." We eat the bread, and we shall never thirst. Is He the bread for eating or for drinking? It seems that John 4 is only about drinking and that John 6 is only about eating. Yet even in John 6, which is apparently a chapter only on eating, there is also a word about drinking. You cannot separate eating from drinking or drinking from eating. Isaiah 55:1 says, "Ho!

Everyone who thirsts, come to the waters... / Come, buy and eat." We come to the waters and obtain food. This proves that the eating and the drinking are just one thing. In our daily life it is hard for any of us to eat without drinking. Have you ever had a meal where you ate without drinking? Eating and drinking always go together. These two are one.

The Gospel of John reveals life to us. This life can only be maintained by the life supply, which is food and water. Since we have received the Lord Jesus as our life, we all have to learn how to drink and eat. The reason why so many Christians are weak today is because few know how to eat and drink. Most Christians know that Christ is the bread of life, but few know the way to eat. Many know that Christ is the water of life, but few know the way to drink. We need to be those who not only know how to eat and drink, but who are daily and even hourly eating and drinking. By eating the bread and drinking the water, we not only receive life but also obtain the life supply.

In chapter after chapter of the Gospel of John, the Lord reveals Himself as our life and life supply. We receive Him as our life and partake of Him as our life supply by eating and drinking Him. In chapter 1 the Lord, as the almighty God in the beginning, became flesh, became a man, to be the Lamb of God to accomplish God's redemption for us so that He may be our life. As our life He is also the feast to us with the wine for us to drink and enjoy in chapter 2. The way for us to receive this wine according to chapter 3 is to be born anew. The day we received the Lord Jesus, we were born again, and we began to drink Christ as the wine and enjoy His life as a feast. Now we must drink and eat Christ, realizing that the food and drink are mingled together. Day by day we must drink and eat, and eat and drink, enjoying the Lord all the time.

EATING AND DRINKING
IN THE EPISTLES AND REVELATION

The thought and the concept of eating and drinking is not only in the Gospels but also in the Epistles of the apostles Paul and Peter and in the book of Revelation. In 1 Corinthians 3:2 Paul said, "I gave you milk to drink." On the one hand, milk is drink, and on the other hand, it is food. Milk is food and water together. It is water with food. In 1 Corinthians 10 Paul also spoke about drinking and eating, applying the type of the children of Israel to us (vv. 3-4, 6).

In Hebrews 5 Paul told the saints that they had need of milk and not of solid food because milk is for infants, while solid food is for the full-grown (vv. 12-14). To drink is to take liquid food, and to eat is to take solid food. The weaker you are, the more you need to drink, and the stronger you are, the more you need to eat. Furthermore, when we are sick, we drink more than we eat. When we are healthy, we eat more than we drink. In 1 Corinthians 3 Paul indicated that the saints in Corinth were still very weak. Therefore, he could not feed them with solid food. He could only feed them with milk, liquid food. First Peter 2:2-3 says, "As newborn babes, long for the guileless milk of the word in order that by it you may grow unto salvation, if you have tasted that the Lord is good."

Finally, in Revelation the promises to those who overcome are to eat the tree of life (2:7), to enjoy the hidden manna (v. 17), and to dine with the Lord (3:20). The mention of the tree of life refers back to Genesis 2, and the hidden manna refers to the entire history of the children of Israel in the wilderness. For forty years they ate manna (Exo. 16:35); therefore, manna was the central point of their history. In Revelation 3:20 the Lord Jesus said, "Behold, I stand at the door and knock; if anyone hears My voice and opens the door, then I will come in to him and dine with him and he with Me." To dine is not merely to eat one food but to eat the riches of a meal. This may refer to the eating of the rich produce of the good land of Canaan by the children of Israel (Josh. 5:10-12).

In Revelation 7 the redeemed saints who have been raptured to the heavens, to the presence of God, will enjoy the Lord Jesus as the Lamb and Shepherd, who guides them to springs of waters of life (v. 17). Shepherding includes feeding; therefore, we will eat as well as drink. I do not fully know what we shall do in eternity, but I do know that we will do at least three things—eat, drink, and praise. In eternity eating, drinking, and praising will be our living and our life. Our life in eternity will be an eating, drinking, and praising life. In the local churches we have a foretaste today. We must eat, drink, and praise. When we say, "O Lord, Amen," this is our eating. To say "Hallelujah" is our drinking and praising. Praise the Lord! We are the eating, drinking, and praising people.

Ultimately, in Revelation 22 we are invited to freely drink of the water of life (v. 17). The Spirit and the bride together say to come and drink of the water of life freely. In the entire Bible, Revelation 22:17 is the last call given by God to the human race. This last divine call is to come and drink. If you come to drink, you will surely eat. In the water of life grows the tree of life (v. 2). When we come to the water, we have the tree. When we drink the water, we eat the tree of life. Eating and drinking is the central thought in God's economy. We all must learn how to enjoy the divine life by eating and drinking Christ.

CHAPTER NINE

THE BREATH OF LIFE

Scripture Reading: Gen. 2:7; Ezek. 37:1-14, 26-28; John 20:22;
3:8; Acts 2:2, 4; 2 Tim. 3:16; Rev. 11:11; 2 Thes. 2:8

THE FOOD IN THE WATER AND
THE WATER IN THE AIR

In the previous chapters we have seen that the Lord is our
life supply as water for us to drink and as food for us to eat.
We have also seen that the food is in the water. Isaiah 55 tells
us that when we come to the waters, we eat. The tree of life as
the food grows in the water of life. Thus, if we are going to eat
the tree of life, we have to come to the water of life. We must
come to the water to get our food. Isaiah 55:1 tells us that
when we come to the waters we eat, and we "buy wine and
milk without money and without price." It is hard to say
whether milk is water or food because milk is food in water.
Wine is the same in principle as milk; it is food in water. Wine
is made from grapes, which are food. When the grapes become
wine, they are food in water.

The food is in the water, and the water is in the air. When
water becomes vapor, it gets into the air. The air sends water
to the earth in the form of rain, and the water on the earth
vaporizes and goes back to the air. There are devices called
vaporizers which convert the water into vapor for inhalation.
After a certain time the water in the vaporizer goes into the
air. When we stay in a room where a vaporizer is being used,
we breathe in the air and get the water because the water is
in the air.

Genesis 2:5-6 says, "No plant of the field was yet in the
earth, and no herb of the field had yet sprung up—for Jehovah

God had not caused it to rain upon the earth, and there was
no man to work the ground, but a mist went up from the
earth and watered the whole surface of the ground." The
mist from the earth is the vapor. Plants grow to produce
food by being watered, and the water comes from the air.
The air sends the water, and the water issues in the food.
In Ezekiel 47 we saw that along with the water are the trees
for food. The water heals the Salt Sea and produces many
fish. The water also waters the desert, turning it into fountains of kids and of calves. The trees, the fish, and the cattle
are for food. This food came from the water, and the water
comes from the air.

If we want to get the food, we have to go to the water. If
we are going to get the water, we need the air. If we are going
to eat, we have to drink. If we are going to drink, we have to
breathe. When we breathe in the air, we have the water.
Furthermore, in the water we have the food.

Eventually, the air is the breath, and in the Bible the
breath is the Spirit. In both the Hebrew and Greek languages,
the word for *Spirit* is the same word for *breath.* The Greek
word for *Spirit* is *pneuma,* and the Hebrew word for *Spirit*
is ruach. In Ezekiel 37 this Hebrew word is translated
into three words: *Spirit, breath,* and *wind. Breath* can be
translated into "Spirit" (v. 5), *wind* can be translated into
"breath" (v. 9), and *breath* can be translated into "wind" or
"Spirit" (v. 9).

The food is in the water, the water is in the air, the air
is the breath, the breath is the Spirit, and the Spirit is God.
John 4:24 tells us that God is Spirit. The essence of God is
Spirit. Just as wood may be the essence of a table, Spirit is
the divine essence. God is Spirit; He is *ruach* or *pneuma.* The
essence of God is the divine breath. God is breath to us.
Man was the only item of God's creation into whom God
breathed the breath of life (Gen. 2:7). This breath of life
became man's human spirit. God made man by forming
him out of the dust of the ground and breathing the breath of
life into him. Revelation 11:11 also records an instance of
the breath of life out of God entering into men. Among God's
creatures, only man has this privilege.

FIRE, BREATH, AND WATER

The three main chapters in the book of Ezekiel are chapter 1, chapter 37, and chapter 47. In chapter 1 is the fire, in chapter 37 is the breath, and in chapter 47 is the water. All the worldly and sinful things including Satan and his host are under the burning fire. Eventually, all of these negative things will be put into the lake of fire (Rev. 20:10), but we believers will be the constituents of the city of water, the New Jerusalem (22:1). In between the fire and the water is the breath.

THE DRY BONES IN NEED OF BREATH

In Ezekiel 47 is the house of God, the building of God, but in chapter 37 the Lord's children are pictured as disjointed, dry bones. None of the bones are joined to one another. The bones are independent and separate. These dry bones are in the midst of a valley. The picture here is similar to that of the children of Israel before their exodus from Egypt. The last verse of Genesis shows that the children of Israel were in a "coffin in Egypt" (50:26). In Ezekiel 37 the children of Israel are depicted as being in graves (vv. 12-13). The dry bones scattered in the midst of the valley are the bones of slain people (v. 9b). Satan is the one who killed and buried them. The dry bones are in need of the air, the breath, to bring them to life.

There is an expanse of air around the earth that life may exist on this earth to serve God's purpose. As the Spirit, God is the real air, the breath. In the air is the water, and in the water is the food. God as life to us is our air, our water, and our food. When we breathe, we drink, and when we drink, we eat. The eating is in the drinking, and the drinking is in the breathing. Furthermore, the breathing is in the praising. When we say, "O Lord! Amen! Hallelujah!" we breathe. The way to breathe in our wonderful Lord is to say, "O Lord! Amen! Hallelujah!" As we breathe in the Lord in this way, we are watered, and our thirst is quenched. We have the sense that we are filled and satisfied. We can breathe, drink, and eat the Lord by calling, "O Lord! Amen! Hallelujah!" By saying, "O Lord! Amen! Hallelujah!" we get the air, the water, and the food.

Hymns, #255 by A. B. Simpson is a wonderful hymn on breathing. The chorus of this hymn says,

> I am breathing out my sorrow,
>   Breathing out my sin;
> I am breathing, breathing, breathing,
>   All Thy fulness in.

We need to breathe Christ in as our breath. We can receive Christ into our inward parts by breathing Him in.

THE WIND, THE BREATH, AND THE SPIRIT

We need to remember that in Ezekiel 37 the wind is the breath, and the breath is the Spirit. Verse 9 says, "Then He said to me, Prophesy to the wind; prophesy, son of man, and say to the wind, Thus says the Lord Jehovah, Come from the four winds, O breath, and breathe on these slain, that they may live." The Lord told Ezekiel to say to the wind, "O breath." This means that the wind is the breath. The *wind* and the *breath* in this verse are the Hebrew word *ruach.* Then verse 14 says, "I will put My Spirit in you." *Spirit* in this verse is also *ruach.* Thus, the wind is the breath, and the breath is the Spirit. When the Lord blows, He is the wind. When we breathe Him, He is the breath. When He gets into us, He is the Spirit. The Lord comes as the wind, we receive Him as the breath, He gets into us as the Spirit, and the Spirit is life.

THE BONES COMING TOGETHER
WITH NOISE AND SHAKING

Before the Spirit came, we were dry bones. We were not only slain and dried up, but we were also buried in graves and in the valley. After Ezekiel's prophesying, "There was a noise, and suddenly, a rattling; and the bones came together, bone to its bone" (v. 7). Before Ezekiel's prophecy the dry bones were quiet and separate. A cemetery full of dried and buried bones is a quiet place. Our meetings, however, should not be like a cemetery. When we come together, there should be "noise and rattling." When the Spirit as the wind blows upon us, how could we be silent? Our meetings should be full of the proper noise. There should be a proper noise where everyone speaks, everyone prays, everyone praises, and everyone gives thanks. The Psalms tell us to make a joyful noise unto the Lord (66:1; 81:1; 95:1-2; 98:4, 6; 100:1).

After the bones came together, "there were sinews on them, and flesh came back, and skin covered them over; but there was no breath in them" (Ezek. 37:8). After the bones came together, the sinews, flesh, and skin covered them. This covering caused their appearance to be much better. Formerly, they were only dry bones, but now they were a body without breath. It is the marvelous doing of the Lord that the bones could come together without life in them.

We have to interpret Ezekiel 37 in a spiritual way. Before God came in to renew us and regenerate us, we were like dead and dry bones. God's salvation is not merely for sinful people but for dead people. Because we were dead and dry, we were also scattered. Whether we were unsaved sinners or backslidden believers, our situation was that we were dead and buried in a grave. Many Christians are dead and dry, scattered and disjointed. They are not connected to anyone. The Lord came in to rescue us through the prophesying of His word. As Ezekiel prophesied, the bones came together, and the sinews, the flesh, and the skin covered them.

THE BREATH OF LIFE COMING INTO THE DRY BONES TO ACCOMPLISH GOD'S PURPOSE

These bones needed a further prophecy so that the breath of life could come into them. When Ezekiel prophesied again, "The breath came into them; and they lived and stood up upon their feet, an exceedingly great army" (v. 10). The bones first became a body. Then the breath came into the bones, and they lived. When they stood up, they became an exceedingly great army to fight the battle for God. The bones become the army fighting the battle, and eventually they become the habitation for God's dwelling to express God. The army is for the dominion to deal with God's enemy, and the dwelling place is for the expression, the image, of God. Through the breathing of the Spirit, God is expressed, and His enemy is dealt with.

Ezekiel prophesies twice in chapter 37. The first time he prophesies to the bones and the second time to the wind. First, he prophesies to the dead ones, and second, he prophesies to the Spirit. The Lord charged Ezekiel to prophesy a second time and say, "Come from the four winds, O breath, and breathe on these slain, that they may live" (v. 9). Then the bones that were formed into a body received the breath of life. They stood up upon their feet and were formed into an army to fight the battle for God. This also gave God the ground to build them together as His habitation. The army and the house fulfill God's twofold purpose to deal with His enemy and to express Him in His image. Image and dominion are brought in by the breathing of the Spirit.

THE BREATH OF LIFE IN THE NEW TESTAMENT

In the New Testament, the Gospel of John tells us that the Lord Jesus came back on the evening of His resurrection to the disciples (20:19). He breathed into them and told them to receive the holy pneuma (v. 22). Again, the word *pneuma* may be translated into "Spirit" or "breath." The Lord breathed into the disciples and told them to receive the holy breath. Today the Lord in His resurrection is the breath of life, the Spirit of life. In John 3 the Lord Jesus told Nicodemus that the Spirit is like the wind, which blows where it wills and cannot be seen but can be realized by its sound (v. 8). On the day of Pentecost, "there was a sound out of heaven, as of a rushing violent wind" (Acts 2:2). This rushing violent wind was the blowing of the Spirit, the blowing of the heavenly *ruach* or *pneuma*.

Revelation 11:11 tells us that the two witnesses, after being dead for three and a half days, were resurrected by the breath of life out of God entering into them. The breath of life will come into the two witnesses and resurrect them during the time of the great tribulation. Second Thessalonians 2:8 tells us that when the Lord Jesus comes back, He will slay the Antichrist by the breath of His mouth, the Spirit. The breath of life gives life to us but kills the lawless one.

Second Timothy 3:16 tells us that all Scripture is God-breathed. This indicates that the Scripture, the Word of God, is the breath of God. God's speaking is God's breathing. God is breath to us. In this breath is the water, and in this water is the food. If we are going to enjoy God as food, we have to drink Him as the water. To drink Him as the water, we have to breathe Him as our breath. By breathing in the Lord, we drink Him and we eat Him. We can drink Him anywhere and eat Him anywhere because we can breathe Him in anywhere. Our spiritual food and drink are available to us at any time and in any place. Physically speaking, we can breathe everywhere, but we cannot drink and eat everywhere. But spiritually speaking, we can eat and drink everywhere because our spiritual eating is in our drinking, and the drinking is in the breathing. When we receive the Lord as the divine air, we enjoy Him as the living water and the heavenly food.

CHAPTER TEN

THE SEED OF LIFE

Scripture Reading: Gen. 1:11-12, 29; Luke 8:5-8a, 11-15; Matt.
13:4-8, 19-24, 31, 33, 37-38, 44-46; 1 Cor. 3:6-12; 1 Pet. 1:23;
James 1:18; Rev. 14:4b, 15

Thus far, we have covered three aspects of life: the tree of
life, the river of life, and the breath of life. The tree of life is
for eating, the river of life is for drinking, and the breath of
life is for breathing. To maintain life we need air, water, and
food. Air is the first item of importance in the maintenance of
life, water is second, and food is third. A person can fast without eating or drinking but not without breathing. If we
graduate from breathing, we graduate from life and die. We
have seen that food comes from water, and water comes from
the air. Thus, the air is the most basic item for maintaining
life.

In this chapter we want to see the fourth aspect of life, the
aspect of the seed of life. This aspect is much deeper than
the other three aspects. We need to be those who know what
life is. Many so-called Bible teachers cannot give any practical help in the matter of life because they themselves are not
clear about what life is. They may have many teachings, but
they have never been impressed with the things of life. The
Bible shows us the tree of life, the river of life, the breath of
life, and the seed of life. The tree is food to eat, the river is
water to drink, the breath is air to breathe, and the seed is a
container of life. The life essence, or germ, the begetting
power of life, the growth of life, the transformation of life, and
the resurrection life are all included in the seed of life. The
word *seed* has an all-inclusive meaning since it is the embodiment of life and includes all things related to life.

THE HERB YIELDING SEED AND
THE TREE YIELDING SEED BEING MAN'S FOOD

We have seen that Genesis 1 is not merely a record of creation but a record absolutely of life. Genesis 1:11-12 tells us that the earth brought forth "herbs yielding seed," and verse 29 refers to "every tree which has fruit that produces seed." According to God's original arrangement, He gave only the herb yielding seed and the tree producing seed to man for food. Anything that did not yield seed, God did not give to man for food. Whatever God gave to man for food before the fall was something yielding seed. This is because in God's intention, in God's economy, man should be taking in, receiving, and enjoying life all the time. Man should not eat, or take in, anything that does not yield seed. Whatever man touches, whatever man takes in, whatever man eats, must be something of life and something producing life—something yielding seed.

God has no intention for man to eat anything that is not of life. God has no intention for man to contact anything that does not yield seed. Whatever man contacts, whatever man takes into himself, whatever man eats for his maintenance, must be something yielding seed. Many books that we may read do not yield seed. But many of us who have read the book entitled *The Economy of God* can testify that it yields seed. According to Genesis, what man eats must be something yielding seed. Anything that does not yield seed, he should not eat. The tree of life is a tree yielding seed. In the seed, the main thing is life. The life essence, the life germ, is in the seed, and this life in the seed is for producing. We may also say that the life in the seed is for resurrection, for spreading, for transforming, and for growth. Life is in the seed, and the seed is food to us. In other words, life is in Christ, and Christ is food to us.

THE LORD JESUS BEING THE SEED OF THE WOMAN,
THE SEED OF DAVID, AND THE SEED OF ABRAHAM

In both the Old and New Testaments the Lord Jesus has many titles. Among His many titles, He has the title of *the seed*. In Genesis 3:15 He is the seed of the woman who will bruise the head of the serpent. In 2 Samuel 7 He is the seed of David (v. 12). In Genesis 12 He is the seed of Abraham (v. 7). In the New Testament, Galatians 3 tells us that the seed of Abraham is the Lord Jesus (v. 16). Abraham had two sons, Ishmael and Isaac, but only one seed. Ishmael was a son of Abraham, but he was not the seed. Galatians 3 tells us that the unique seed of Abraham is Christ, of whom Isaac was a type. Isaac was a type of Christ as the seed of Abraham.

THE SEED BEING THE WORD OF GOD, THE SONS OF THE KINGDOM, AND CHRIST HIMSELF

In the Gospels the Lord Jesus likened Himself to a sower sowing the seed. The seed is the word of God (Luke 8:11), the sons of the kingdom (Matt. 13:38), and Christ Himself (1 Pet. 1:23). The word of God is the embodiment of Christ. The word of God being the seed means that the seed is Christ. As the sons of the kingdom, we are also the seed. This means that we are the reproduction of Christ, the unique seed. In John 12:24 the Lord Jesus indicated that He was the unique grain, or seed, who fell into the earth and died. Through the death of the one grain of wheat, many grains are produced. The one grain is Jesus, and we are the many grains. Thus, we are the reproduction of Jesus because the many grains are the reproduction of the one grain. Human words are not adequate to explain the marvelous and deep mystery of the rich, all-inclusive seed of life. We must remember that the word of God, Christ, and we are the seed. We should not have the ambition to be merely Bible teachers, but we have to be seeds for the reproduction of life. The apostle Paul told the Corinthians that he was their father who begot them through the gospel (1 Cor. 4:15).

In 1 Corinthians the apostle Paul used three phrases to describe his relationship with them: *I fed you* (3:2, ASV), *I planted* (v. 6), and *I have begotten you* (4:15). Paul emphasized the fact that he had begotten the Corinthians and that he had planted and fed them. Paul was a father, a farmer, and a feeder. We need to be sowers and seeds in our locality. We have to sow ourselves into the church life in our locality. We have to be those who beget, plant, and feed others. We need to be the seeds with life in them for food. We should not be in our localities to pass on merely teachings or knowledge. We should be there as seeds with life in them, which are good for food to feed others. We need to plant ourselves, sow ourselves, as the seed in our localities. Then we will be fathers and farmers. We will be those who reproduce and bring forth life.

DEALING WITH OUR HEART
FOR THE GROWTH OF THE SEED OF LIFE

Matthew 13 and Luke 8 show us that the Lord came to sow the seed, which is Himself. After being sown into us, the seed of life needs to grow, and its growth needs our cooperation, our coordination. Our cooperation, or coordination, is to have a proper heart. The problem is not with the spirit but with the heart. The heart includes the conscience (Heb. 10:22), the mind (4:12), the emotion (John 16:20), and the will (Acts 11:23). If we are going to coordinate with the growth of the seed within us, we have to deal with our conscience, our mind, our emotion, and our will. If we do not deal with all the parts of our heart, it will be hard for the seed of life to grow within us. The Lord Jesus gave four illustrations of the kind of heart we might have: the wayside, the rocky places, the thorns, and the good earth (Matt. 13:4-8, 19-23; Luke 8:5-8a, 11-15).

The wayside is the outskirts, or the edge, of the field that is close to the way. Because it is so close to the way, it is easily hardened by the traffic of the way. Many unbelievers' and believers' hearts are hardened. The wayside signifies the heart that is hardened by worldly traffic. Our heart may be too close to the traffic of today's world. The seed cannot penetrate such a heart hardened by worldly traffic. The seed can only fall on the surface where the birds, signifying the evil one, Satan, can come and snatch it away. Satan, the evil one in the air (Matt. 13:19), realizes that the seed cannot get into the heart that is like the wayside, so he comes to snatch away the seed. Before farmers sow seed, they generally till the soil to loosen it. But the wayside is hardened, so it is easy for the birds to snatch away the seeds. If our heart is the wayside, it is easy for Satan to come and snatch away the word that was sown in our heart.

The next type of soil is the soil with the rocky places. Matthew 13:5 tells us that this kind of soil lacks "depth of earth." On the surface is the earth, and underneath are the rocks. Underneath the soil of our heart, there may be rocky places. The wayside is hard, but not as hard as rocks. On the surface our heart may appear to be soft, but underneath we may be hardened as rocks. The seed within us may grow and spring up, but it cannot root deep within us because of the rocky places. The ones with a shallow heart and with hidden rocks cannot stand against any temptation or persecution. The rocks may signify hidden sins, personal desires, self-seeking, and self-pity which frustrate the seed from gaining root in the depth of the heart. Luke 8:6 tells us that the seed which fell on the rock sprouted up but withered because it had no moisture. The shallow earth is easily dried up by the heat of the sun. If the earth is deep, the surface may dry up, but there will still be some moisture or water underneath that maintains the growth in life. We all have to go to the Lord and allow Him to examine us so that we may see how deep the earth is within us.

The thorns signify the anxiety of the age, the deceitfulness of riches, and the pleasures of this life that choke the seed (Matt. 13:22; Luke 8:14). These thorns choke the word from growing in the heart and cause it to become unfruitful.

A good heart is a heart that has been thoroughly tilled and is soft toward the Lord. It is a heart that is not hardened by worldly traffic, without hidden sins, without the anxiety of the age, the deceitfulness of riches, and the pleasures this of life. The wayside, the rocky places, and the thorns have to be dealt with thoroughly in order for us to have a good heart. The good heart is a heart with a pure and good conscience, with a considerate and sober mind, with an affectionate yet restricted emotion, and with a softened and flexible will. Such a heart gives every inch of its ground to receive the word that the word may grow, bear fruit, and produce even a hundredfold (Matt. 13:23).

THE SEED OF LIFE, THE GROWTH IN LIFE,
AND THE TRANSFORMATION IN LIFE
IN MATTHEW 13 AND FIRST CORINTHIANS 3

In Matthew 13 the first three parables are parables concerning the seed. The first parable is the sower sowing the seed, the second parable is the sower sowing the good seed (vv. 24-30), and the third parable is the sower sowing the mustard seed (vv. 31-32).

The fourth parable is a parable concerning the produce of the seed—the fine flour (vv. 33-35). This parable tells us that a woman took leaven and hid it within the unleavened fine flour until all of it was leavened. *Leaven* in the Scripture signifies evil things (1 Cor. 5:6, 8) and evil doctrines (Matt. 16:6, 11-12). Fine flour, or the meal, for making the meal offering (Lev. 2:1), signifies Christ as food both to God and man. This woman typifies the Catholic Church, which took many pagan practices, heretical doctrines, and evil matters and mixed them with the teachings concerning Christ to leaven the whole content of Christianity.

The fifth parable is concerning the treasure hidden in the field, and the sixth parable is concerning the merchant who finds the one pearl of great value. The treasure hidden in the field must consist of gold or precious stones, the materials for the building of the church and the New Jerusalem (1 Cor. 3:12; Rev. 21:18-20). The pearl is also the material for the building up of the New Jerusalem (v. 21). Gold, pearl, and precious stones are the issue of the growth of the seed of life. Within the seed is the element of transformation. The issue of the tree of life in Genesis 2:9-12 is gold, pearl (bdellium), and precious stone (onyx stone).

In 1 Corinthians 3:6 Paul said, "I planted, Apollos watered, but God caused the growth." Then he proceeded to reveal that the church is "God's cultivated land, God's building" (v. 9), and that we need to build the church with gold, silver, and precious stones (v. 12). The gold, silver, and precious stones for God's building come from the growth in life in God's cultivated land. The church, the house of God, must be built with gold, silver, and precious stones, precious materials from Christ growing in us. As God's cultivated land, we have

Christ planted in us. Christ must also grow in us and out of us to produce the precious materials of gold, silver, and precious stones for the building of God's habitation on the earth. Both in Matthew 13 and 1 Corinthians 3 there are the concepts of the seed of life, the growth in life, and the transformation in life. The seed of life is sown within us and grows in us to transform us into precious material for God's building.

THE INCORRUPTIBLE SEED, THE FIRSTFRUITS, AND THE HARVEST

Peter tells us that we were regenerated of the incorruptible seed (1 Pet. 1:23). Then James tells us that we were brought forth to be the firstfruits of His creatures (1:18). He regenerated us to be the firstfruits of His new creation by imparting His divine life into our being through the implanted word of life (v. 21).

In Revelation 14 the firstfruits of the believers are raptured before the great tribulation (v. 4b), while the harvest of the believers, who are also raptured, occurs near the end of the great tribulation (v. 15). Out of this harvest come all the precious stones which are good for God's building, the New Jerusalem. Eventually, from the cultivated land comes God's building. We are God's cultivated land and God's building. In Genesis the seed of life is first mentioned, and in Revelation there is the harvest of the seed. In between Genesis and Revelation is the sowing of the seed, the growth of the seed, and the transformation in life from this growth. Thank the Lord for the seed of life.

CHAPTER ELEVEN

THE SPIRIT OF LIFE

(1)

Scripture Reading: John 6:63; 2 Cor. 3:6c; 1 Cor. 15:45b; Rom. 8:2a; John 3:5-6b; 4:24; Matt. 28:18-19

THE SPIRIT WHO GIVES LIFE

We have covered the tree of life, the river of life, the breath of life, and the seed of life. In this chapter we come to the ultimate point, the highest point—the Spirit of life. There are three places in the New Testament that refer to the Spirit as the Spirit who gives life. John 6:63 tells us that it is the Spirit who gives life. Second Corinthians 3:6 tells us that the letter kills, but the Spirit gives life. Finally, 1 Corinthians 15:45 says that the last Adam became a life-giving Spirit. There is a principle in the Bible that two is the number of testimony. To speak something a third time is a confirmation to what has been testified. What has been spoken three times has been spoken in a full way. The matter of the Spirit giving life has been spoken, testified, and confirmed in the New Testament. The Holy Spirit of God is the life-giving Spirit, the Spirit who gives life.

The term *the Spirit of life* is mentioned only once in the New Testament; Romans 8:2 refers to "the law of the Spirit of life...in Christ Jesus." In this verse are four items: the law, the Spirit, life, and Christ. The law is the law of life, the Spirit is the Spirit of life, and Christ is the Christ of life. The law, the Spirit, and Christ are related one to another, and they are one in life. Christ is the life-giving Spirit, and this Spirit is the Spirit of life. Revelation 11:11 tells us that the pneuma of life, the breath of life, comes into the two witnesses, who had been killed by Antichrist. This shows us that the Spirit of life is simply the breath of life.

It is very difficult to define what life is, but thank the Lord that in the Bible we can trace something of the divine life. The divine life is with the Spirit of God. The Spirit of God today is the life-giving Spirit, the Spirit of life, and this Spirit of life is the breath of life. If we have the breath of life, we have the Spirit of life and life itself. It is easy for us to receive life because this life is with the divine breath. We just need to breathe in the divine breath by exercising our spirit, our breathing organ.

FOUR ASPECTS OF THE DIVINE SPIRIT

God Being Spirit

According to the revelation of the New Testament, the divine Spirit has at least four crucial aspects. First, the New Testament says clearly that God is Spirit (John 4:24). John 4:24 does not say that God is *a* Spirit but that God is Spirit. This is similar to saying that a table is wood. *Spirit* in John 4:24 refers to the divine essence just like wood can be the essence of a table.

The Spirit Being the Application of the Triune God

Second, the Bible tells us a mystery which we can never understand adequately, that is, that our God is the Triune God. The word *triune* is not in the Bible, but the fact of God's being triune is revealed in the Bible. In Genesis 1:1 the word *God* is used for the first time. The subject *God* in Hebrew *(Elohim)* is plural in number, whereas the verb in this verse is singular in number. This contains the meaning that God is three-one. Matthew 28:19 tells us to disciple the nations, baptizing them into the name of the Father and of the Son and of the Holy Spirit. This verse uses the singular *name,* not names. There is one name for the Divine Trinity. The name is the sum total of the Divine Being, equivalent to His person.

The Father is in the Son, and the Son with the Father is in

the Spirit. The three persons of the Godhead are not three
separate beings, just as man's spirit, soul, and body are not
three separate parts. A man is one complete being with three
parts. God is triune, and man is tripartite. With God there are
three persons, but we should not think that these three persons are three separate, divine beings. Some Christians
believe that the three of the Godhead are not only distinct but
also separate. While the three of the Godhead are distinct, it
is wrong, according to the truth of the Scriptures, to say that
They are separate. The Father, the Son, and the Spirit are not
three separate gods. Both in the Old Testament and the New
Testament, we are always told that there is only one God
(Isa. 45:5; Psa. 86:10; 1 Cor. 8:4; 1 Tim. 2:5). The Bible tells
us clearly that God is uniquely one but that He is triune
with three persons—the Father, the Son, and the Spirit. God
the Father is in God the Son, and God the Son is in God the
Spirit. In John 14:10 the Lord says that He is in the Father
and the Father is in Him. Furthermore, Romans 8:2 refers to
the Spirit of life in Christ Jesus.

We may also say that the Father is the Son and that the
Son is the Spirit. In Isaiah 9:6 the Son is called Eternal
Father, and 2 Corinthians 3:17 says that the Lord is the
Spirit. On the one hand, the Father is in the Son, and the Son
is in the Spirit. On the other hand, the Father is the Son, and
the Son is the Spirit.

The three of the Godhead are distinct, yet They are one.
John 1:1 says that the Word was with God and that the Word
was God. On the one hand, the Word and God are distinct,
and on the other hand, They are one. Second Corinthians 3:17
says that the Lord is the Spirit, but it also refers to the Spirit
of the Lord. On the one hand, the Lord and the Spirit are one,
but on the other hand, They are distinct.

Now we have to ask why God needs to be triune. To
answer this we need to know the whole Bible in a proper way.
God needs to be triune because He desires to work Himself
into us, to dispense Himself into us. *Dispensation* is the noun
form of the verb *dispense*. God's dispensation is His plan to
dispense Himself into us. God's dispensation, His economy, is
to dispense Himself into us, to apply Himself to us.

Let us take electricity as an illustration of God's dispensing. The current of electricity and electricity itself are not two separate matters. They are one. The current of electricity is the electricity itself in motion. When electricity moves, when it flows, there is the current of electricity. We need the current of electricity for the application of electricity. If we never applied electricity, there would be no need for us to have the current of electricity. But if we are going to dispense electricity into our homes, we need the current of electricity. The current of electricity is for the dispensation, the economy, of electricity.

In the New Testament Jesus told us that He, as the Son, was sent by the Father (John 5:37; 8:18, 29). His being sent by the Father indicates that the Father is the source, out of which the Son flowed to be among mankind. This does not mean that the Son and the Father were two separate divine beings substantially. They are substantially one Divine Being. The Father is the source, and the Son is the expression of the Father. But the Son as the expression of the Father could only come to be among mankind; He could not come into man. Thus, we need the Spirit. In John 14 the Lord Jesus indicated that He needed to change His form from the flesh into the Spirit. He indicated that He had to pass through death and enter into resurrection so that He could come into us as the Spirit, as the breath (vv. 16-20). After His death and resurrection, He came back as the breath of life. In the evening on the day of resurrection, He came to the disciples, breathed into them, and said, "Receive the Holy Spirit" (20:22). As the breath He got into the disciples, so God was dispensed into human beings. Thus, the Divine Trinity is for God's dispensation to dispense God into us.

The Spirit is the final person of God's dispensation and of God's visitation. How could God come to us? How could God visit us? He comes to us and visits us as the Spirit. Electricity comes into a room as the current. If there is no current of electricity, the electricity cannot be dispensed into the room and be applied to it. Electricity is applied to us in its current. Thus, the current is the visitation of electricity. In like manner, the Spirit is the visitation of God, the dispensing of God, the application of God. The third person of the Godhead, who is the Spirit, is the application of God to us. If God is going to be applied to us, He needs to be the Spirit. The essence of God needs the application of God. The essence of a certain medicine needs to be put in the form of a pill so that it can be dispensed into a sick patient. The pill is for the application of the medicine. Likewise, the Spirit as the third person of the Godhead is for God's application of His essence to dispense Himself into us.

The Life-giving Spirit

Now we want to see the third aspect of the divine Spirit. The first aspect is that God is Spirit in essence, and the second aspect is that God in His Trinity is the Spirit for application. The third aspect of the divine Spirit can be seen in 1 Corinthians 15:45, which tells us that the last Adam, who was Christ in the flesh, became a life-giving Spirit. The Redeemer, the Savior, who passed through incarnation, human living, crucifixion, resurrection, and ascension, became a life-giving Spirit. The third aspect of the divine Spirit is the aspect of life-giving. The essence is for the application, and the application is for life-giving. The Lord wants to apply Himself into us to give us life.

The Word Being the Spirit

The fourth aspect of the divine Spirit is that the words the Lord speaks to us are spirit (John 6:63). This shows that His spoken words are the embodiment of the life-giving Spirit. God is Spirit, the third person of the Godhead is Spirit, Christ was made a life-giving Spirit, and the divine word is Spirit. This is one Spirit in four aspects. The first aspect is the essence, the second is the application, the third is the life-giving, and the fourth is the word for feeding. John 6 tells us that Christ is the bread of life to feed us (vv. 35, 57). We need the essence and the application for life-giving, and this life-giving mostly depends upon feeding. The Lord feeds us with Himself as the bread of life. The Spirit is living and real but rather abstract, mysterious, intangible, and difficult for people to apprehend. But the words are substantial and concrete.

It is the Spirit who gives life, and today the Spirit is embodied in the word. The Spirit today is consolidated into the word, the living word. *Words* in Greek in John 6:63 is not *logos* but *rhema*—the instant, living, present, up-to-date word.

THE ALL-INCLUSIVE SPIRIT FOR THE DISPENSING OF GOD INTO US AS OUR LIFE AND LIFE SUPPLY

The four aspects of the divine Spirit that we have seen are for one purpose—to dispense God into us as our life and as our life supply. God Himself is Spirit essentially, the last person of the Godhead is the Spirit economically, Christ is the Spirit all-inclusively, and the words that He speaks are the Spirit practically for the one purpose of giving us life and feeding us with God Himself. These four aspects are like four steps that God takes to dispense Himself into us as life. The Spirit of life includes God as Spirit; includes the third person of God's Trinity; includes the all-inclusive, redeeming Christ with His incarnation, human living, crucifixion, resurrection, and ascension; and includes the living word of God. All that God is to us is the all-inclusive Spirit, which is the Spirit of life. This Spirit gives us life. As a help in realizing the all-inclusiveness of the Spirit of life, I would encourage you to read the booklet entitled *The All-inclusive Spirit of Christ* (see *The Collected Works of Witness Lee,* 1965, Vol. 1).

CHAPTER TWELVE

THE SPIRIT OF LIFE

(2)

Scripture Reading: John 3:5-6; Rom. 8:2, 9, 15, 23; 1 Cor. 12:13; 2 Cor. 3:17-18; 13:14; Gal. 5:22, 25; Eph. 3:16; 4:23; Titus 3:5-6; Phil. 1:19; 2 Thes. 2:13; 1 John 2:27

In the last chapter we saw four aspects of the divine Spirit, the all-inclusive Spirit of life, for the dispensing of God Himself as life into our being. In this chapter we want to see more aspects of the Spirit of life.

THE BEGETTING SPIRIT

John 3:5-6 tells us that the Spirit of life is the begetting Spirit. To be born again is to be born of the Spirit of life. "That which is born of the Spirit is spirit" (v. 6). The Spirit of life brings Christ with the divine life into us, and we are born again. Then this begetting Spirit begins to dwell within us as the Spirit of life.

THE LAW OF THE SPIRIT OF LIFE

The term *the Spirit of life* is mentioned only in Romans 8:2. This Spirit of life has a law. A law regulates. The law is not only a regulating matter but is also a power, an energy, and a spontaneous strength. A grain of wheat grows out wheat, and a peach tree brings forth peaches because there is a life law. This life law regulates. There is no need for a person to regulate the peach tree and tell it, "Peach tree, you should not bring forth apples. If you bring forth apples, you will be punished." There is no need to teach the peach tree in this way because within the peach life is the peach law.

The life law regulates the peach tree so that it brings forth only peaches. Within the life law there is the spontaneous power, the strength, and the energy to produce something according to the regulating law.

Scientists investigate the laws that operate in nature, such as the law of gravity and the law of aerodynamics. I think the apostle Paul was the greatest "scientist" because he discovered the law of the Spirit of life. Within the life of the Spirit is a law. With every life there is a law. Dogs bark according to the law of the dog life, and chickens lay eggs according to the law of the chicken life. We have the divine life, the life of the Spirit, and with this life there is also a law. This law regulates us from within and is powerful and spontaneous. This law sets us free from another law, a negative law, the law of sin and of death.

The law of gravity works to pull things down to the earth. By my effort, I may hold a book in the air with an outstretched arm, but eventually my effort will be exhausted. Because of the law of gravity, I will have to put the book down. A higher law is needed to overcome the law of gravity. Similarly, we need a higher law to overcome the law of sin and of death. As believers in Christ, we have this higher, positive law, the law of life, which is versus the negative law, the law of sin and of death. The unbelievers do not have this positive law within them, only the negative one. We have another law within us because we have another life, the divine life. With this life is the divine law that sets us free from the law of sin and of death.

THE SPIRIT OF GOD AND THE SPIRIT OF CHRIST

Romans 8:9 tells us that the Spirit is the Spirit of God and also the Spirit of Christ. We may say that *the Spirit of God* and *the Spirit of Christ* are synonyms, but there is still some difference between these terms. The Spirit of God brings us the essence of all that God is with all God's attributes. But the Spirit of Christ brings us all that Christ is. God is Christ, and Christ is God. But Christ is both God and man. We cannot say that God is God and man, but we can say that Christ is God and man. The Spirit of Christ is the Spirit not only of God but also of man. God is the Creator, but Christ, as both God and man, is the Redeemer.

We may say that the Spirit of God is the Spirit of Christ and that the Spirit of Christ is the Spirit of God. But the Spirit of God does not include as much as the Spirit of Christ does. The Spirit of God and the Spirit of Christ are one Spirit but in different stages. The Spirit of God is in the first stage, while the Spirit of Christ is in the second stage. The Spirit of God has the element of divinity and was active in God's creation (Gen. 1:2b). In the Spirit of Christ we have Christ's incarnation, humanity, human living, death, and resurrection. In the Spirit of God there is life, but in the Spirit of Christ there is life as well as resurrection. The Spirit of Christ dwells within us not only as God but also as Christ and comprises the divine nature of God and the human nature, incarnation, human living, crucifixion, and resurrection of Christ.

THE SPIRIT OF SONSHIP

Romans 8:15 tells us that we "have received a spirit of sonship in which we cry, Abba, Father!" The sonship includes the life of the Son, the nature of the Son, the title right of the Son, the position of the Son, the reality of the Son, the potential of the Son, the image of the Son, and the heritage of the Son. Today we are sons of God but not the sons in fullness. The Spirit of sonship will make us real sons in fullness. We may say that we have the life of the Son of God, but this life has not been developed in us to its fullness. We may have the nature of the Son of God, but it is still so hidden. We may have the potential to be rich in Christ, but we may still be poor in the experience and riches of Christ. However, the Spirit of sonship will bring forth in us all the things related to the sonship.

THE FIRSTFRUITS OF THE SPIRIT

Romans 8:23 says that we have the firstfruits of the Spirit. Any fruit comes out of the life seed. The fruit is the outcome of the life within the seed. Thus, the Spirit is not only the life but also the fruit of life. The firstfruits are the foretaste. We have the foretaste, the firstfruits, of the Spirit, and we are waiting for the harvest. According to Romans 8:23 the harvest is the redemption of our body. We have been redeemed in our spirit yet not in our body. Regardless of how much we are in the spirit, sometimes our body really bothers us. My spirit may be strong, yet my body may be weak. Because our body has not yet been redeemed, it is a restriction and limitation to us. If our body is weak or sick, we have to pay attention to its demands. Paul said that we who have the firstfruits of the Spirit are "eagerly awaiting sonship, the redemption of our body" (v. 23). Through the regeneration of our spirit, we have the Spirit as a foretaste. The Spirit is the firstfruits in our spirit. Then we need the harvest of the Spirit, which is the full sonship, the redemption of our body.

DRINKING OF THE SPIRIT

First Corinthians 12:13 says, "In one Spirit we were all baptized into one Body, whether Jews or Greeks, whether slaves or free, and were all given to drink one Spirit." In this verse the Spirit is not only the baptizing water but also the drinking water. We all have been made to drink of the Spirit, and to drink of the Spirit is a life matter. To be baptized is to be put into water, but to drink is to take water into us. After being baptized in the Spirit, we are now drinking of the Spirit. To be baptized in the Spirit is to get into the Spirit and be lost in Him; to drink the Spirit is to take the Spirit in and have our being saturated with Him.

THE BOUNTIFUL SUPPLY OF THE SPIRIT

Philippians 1:19 refers to "the bountiful supply of the Spirit of Jesus Christ." The Spirit supplies us with whatever we need. If we need life, He supplies life. If we need strength, He supplies strength. If we need patience, He supplies patience. If we need the power to endure suffering, the suffering strength, He supplies it. Whatever we need is in the bountiful supply of the Spirit. W. J. Conybeare tells us that the word for *bountiful supply* in Greek literally means the supplying of all the needs of the chorus by the choragus. The choragus was the leader of the chorus, and he met all the needs of everyone in the chorus, such as the needs for food, clothing, lodging, and musical instruments. Whatever the members of the chorus needed, the leader of the chorus supplied. The supply of the choragus truly was bountiful, even all-inclusive. Thank the Lord that whatever we need, the all-inclusive, bountiful Spirit supplies.

THE LIBERATING SPIRIT

Second Corinthians 3:17 tells us that the Lord is the Spirit and "where the Spirit of the Lord is, there is freedom." This means that the Spirit is the liberating Spirit. Where life is, there is always liberation. The more we grow in life, the more we become liberated. The more mature we become in life, the more we are freed from all kinds of bondage. Many of the young saints are still under much bondage. Seemingly they are more free than the saints who are more mature in the divine life, but actually they are more bound. Many of us are bound by religion and religious practices, so we need to experience more of the liberating Spirit. As we grow in life, we are released from our bondage.

The many habits that we have according to our flesh and our natural constitution are bondages. The liberating Spirit can free us from the bondage of our habits. Some brothers have the habit of being silent, while other brothers have the habit of talking all the time. You may want to say something to a brother who has the habit of talking, but you may not get the chance because of his habit. We all need to be liberated from our habits. Another brother may have the habit of speaking softly in a large meeting of the saints. He may be bound by his natural habit and not experience the boldness in the Lord and the release of the spirit. He needs to be liberated from this habit; otherwise, he will not be able to minister adequately. He needs the liberating Spirit to grant him the boldness and the release of the spirit.

When we pray-read the Word, we must be liberated from our habit. We need to pray-read according to the need and the atmosphere. If four or five brothers come together to pray-read the Word in someone's apartment, there is no need for them to shout. If one of the brothers does shout, this is according to his habit. We should shout not according to our habit but according to the situation, the condition, the environment, and the atmosphere. We need the release of our spirit, not the release of our habit. Another brother may have the habit of being quiet all the time. His "exercise of the spirit" fits in the homes of the saints. But when he comes to a meeting of three or four hundred people, he needs the boldness to release his spirit in a living way. In a larger meeting it will be easier for this brother to remain in his habit and to pray-read with the release of his habit of being quiet.

We need the liberation of the Spirit so that we may fit in any kind of environment or situation. With a small number we need to experience the Spirit to pray-read in a low voice. With a large number of saints we need to pray-read with a loud voice in the Spirit. If we are enjoying the liberating Spirit, we will speak when there is a need to speak and be quiet when we need to be quiet. What we do should not be according to our habit but according to the liberation of the Spirit. To enjoy the liberation of the Spirit to the uttermost, we need the growth in life. Outward regulations will not work to deliver us from our habits. The more we grow in life, the more we will be liberated.

THE TRANSFORMING SPIRIT

Second Corinthians 3:18 says, "We all with unveiled face, beholding and reflecting like a mirror the glory of the Lord, are being transformed into the same image from glory to glory, even as from the Lord Spirit." In this verse the Spirit is the transforming Spirit. Transformation is a change in life, a metabolic change. The more life supply we enjoy, the more we will be changed, or transformed. Transformation is not an outward change by some method but an inward change by the supply of life. The transformation mentioned in 2 Corinthians 3:18 is not something of teaching but something of the changing life.

We all need to be changed, not by outward teachings and outward regulations but by the inward growing of life. When little children grow in their human life, they change in appearance from year to year. With the growth in life, there is a change. We all need to pursue the real growth in life, and we all need to have a real change in life. We are not practicing religion, but as the church we are God's cultivated land. We have to take care of the growth in life so that we may have the transformation in life by the Lord Spirit.

THE LORD SPIRIT

Verse 17 of 2 Corinthians 3 tells us that the Lord is the Spirit, and then it refers to the Spirit of the Lord. To say "the Spirit of the Lord" is similar to saying "the current of electricity." The current and the electricity are not two things. In like manner, the Spirit and the Lord are not two different items. The current of electricity is the electricity itself, and the Spirit of the Lord is the Lord Himself. The current of electricity is the electricity itself in motion. The Spirit is the Triune God in motion, the reaching of the Triune God. The Triune God reaches the tripartite man as the Spirit. In verse 18 there is the term *the Lord Spirit*. This is a compound title like *the Father God* and *the Lord Christ*. The compound title *the Father God* refers to the Father who is God or to the very God who is our Father. *The Lord Spirit* refers to the Lord who is the Spirit and to the Spirit who is our Lord. The Lord and the Spirit are not two, but They are one.

In 2 Corinthians 3:17-18 the Spirit is mentioned in three aspects: (1) the Lord is the Spirit, (2) the Spirit of the Lord, and (3) the Lord Spirit. We have to realize that the Lord is the Spirit to us, and we should call Him the Lord Spirit. To call Him the Lord Spirit is according to the subjective experience of life. If we do not know the divine life, it will be difficult for us to call our Lord Jesus the Lord Spirit. As we are experiencing the divine life in our daily life, we will spontaneously have the sense that the Lord is the Spirit. The more we experience the Lord in life, the more we will realize that the Lord is the Spirit to us.

When we experience the divine life in the Spirit and come to the Bible with this experience, we will be able to receive the proper, enlightened understanding from the Word. If we do not have the knowledge or experience of a certain piece of machinery, we will not be able to understand it. If you gave me a part from a car, I would not know what part it is or where to put it. But if you gave the same part to a mechanic, he would know what the part is and know where it belongs. Because he has the knowledge and experience of an automobile, it is easy for him to understand its parts. In the same way, in order to understand the Bible, especially concerning life and the Spirit, we need the real experiences of life and the Spirit. We may learn doctrines, teachings, and theology, but to understand the things concerning life and the Spirit, we need to enjoy and experience Christ as the Lord Spirit. We need to enjoy the liberating Spirit and the transforming Spirit, who transforms us from one degree of glory to another.

CHAPTER THIRTEEN

THE SPIRIT OF LIFE

(3)

Scripture Reading: Titus 3:5; Eph. 4:23; 2 Thes. 2:13; 1 John
2:27; Gal. 5:22, 25; John 14:17; 16:13-15; 2 Cor. 13:14

In chapter 12 we saw something concerning the Spirit of
life in Romans, 1 Corinthians, and 2 Corinthians. In this
chapter we want to continue our fellowship concerning the
Spirit of life.

THE RENEWING SPIRIT

Titus 3:5 refers to the renewing of the Holy Spirit. Transforming and renewing are very much related to one another
(Rom. 12:2). The more we are transformed, the more we are
renewed. The more we are renewed, the more we are transformed. We have pointed out that transformation is not
merely an outward change but an inward change of life, a
metabolic change. Transformation is a very subjective change
from within by life. The renewing of the Spirit is also not an
outward renewing but an inward renewing of life. The divine
life that is imparted into us renews us.

Everything related to our natural being is old. Ephesians 4
tells us that we need to put off the old man, be renewed in the
spirit of our mind, and put on the new man (vv. 22-24). No
matter how young a person is, his very being, the created and
fallen man, is old. The old man is the man of the old creation
which is in Adam. Even a little babe has an old man that
needs to be renewed. Our mind is an old mind, our nature is
an old nature, and our life is an old life.

Adam became old immediately after the fall. The old man

is of Adam, created by God, but fallen through sin. Because of our inherited oldness from Adam, we need to be renewed with all the items of God. Whatever God is and whatever God has is new. Whatever we are and whatever we have is old. God is very ancient because He is infinite, but He is never old. He is ancient yet always new. Because we are so old, we need to be renewed by our new God.

To be renewed means to be replaced. Our mind has to be replaced by the mind of Christ, our nature has to be replaced by the nature of Christ, and our life has to be replaced by the life of Christ. Whatever we have is old. Whatever Christ is, is new. When Christ comes in to replace all that we have and all that we are, He renews us. We need to be renewed with all that Christ is in the way of life. A dentist may replace a person's teeth with some false teeth, but this is not the renewing of a person's teeth, because they are not replaced in the way of life. The Spirit of life renews us in the way of life with all that Christ is.

THE SANCTIFYING SPIRIT

The New Testament tells us that we were sanctified by the blood of Christ (Heb. 13:12; 10:29). Even the Old Testament has the thought that the redeeming blood can sanctify us (Heb. 9:13; cf. Lev. 16:18-19). Sanctification by the blood is merely a change in position and condition outwardly, not a change in disposition inwardly. Before we were saved, we were one among many unsanctified sinners. When we confessed our sins and accepted Christ as our Savior, the blood of Christ sprinkled us and sanctified us, changing our position. The blood separated us from the sinful people in the world. We were sanctified unto God positionally by the blood of Christ.

Before we were saved, our condition was that we were under God's condemnation. But by the Lord's blood, which has been sprinkled upon us, our condition has also been changed. We are no longer under God's condemnation, but we have been justified in the eyes of God by the blood of Christ (Rom. 5:16, 18; 3:24-25). Our condition is now one of justification, not one of condemnation. The blood of Christ has changed our position and our condition before God. We have been justified and reconciled to God.

The blood, however, does not change what we are in our nature, in our disposition. This is why we need another aspect of sanctification. We not only need the outward sanctification by the blood, but we also need the inward sanctification by the Spirit. Second Thessalonians 2:13 speaks of the sanctification of the Spirit. Sanctification in this verse is something in life. The Spirit sanctifies us subjectively and inwardly by changing our disposition. The Holy Spirit sanctifies us inwardly in our disposition with the substance of Christ, with what Christ is, with the essence of God.

A good illustration of dispositional sanctification is the making of tea. When a tea bag is placed into plain water, it "teaifies" the water. When the tea bag is placed in the plain water and remains there for a period of time, the plain water becomes the same in essence, in nature, in appearance, in color, and in odor as the tea. The plain water becomes one with the tea because the tea gets into the water. The more the tea gets into the water, the more the water is teaified. Just as the plain water is teaified, we need to be sanctified, or "Christified." The Holy Spirit comes into us to sanctify us with Christ, to Christify us. The Spirit puts more and more of Christ into us so that we become mingled with Christ just as the tea is mingled with the water. If the tea bag remains in the water for a long time, the teaification becomes intensified. We need to allow Christ to dispense Himself into us in a full way so that we are sanctified, or Christified, in an intensified way.

Romans 6:19 tells us that we need to present our members "as slaves to righteousness unto sanctification." Holiness is the essence of God's divine being. John Wesley interpreted holiness as sinless perfection, a perfection without sin. Holiness, however, is not sinless perfection. The way God makes us holy is to impart Himself, the Holy One, into us so that our whole being may be permeated and saturated with His holy nature.

To purify water and to teaify it are two different things. If you are going to serve me a cup of tea, you may purify the water first and then teaify it. Purification is included in teaification, but purification is not teaification. In like manner, sinless perfection is included in holiness, but sinless perfection is not holiness.

People who are under the concept that sinless perfection is holiness put themselves under many regulations. They may have outward regulations concerning their dress and conduct in order to make themselves "holy." When I was a young Christian, I met with a group of Brethren believers who were very strict. The men had to cut their hair very short. If your hair was very short, you were considered a most spiritual person. Furthermore, the sisters were not supposed to wear anything modern. They all had to wear old-fashioned clothing. One day I realized that the unsaved people who lived in the countryside in China had the same outward practice that we did. The men cut their hair very short, and the women all wore old-fashioned clothes. Seemingly, they were as "spiritual" as we were. It was then that I realized that the teaching of holiness as sinless perfection was wrong.

Holiness is God's divine essence, the essence of God's divine being. For water to become tea, the substance of tea must be placed into the water. Holiness is when we are "teaified" with God as the divine tea. When something of God's divine being is dispensed into us, we are sanctified; that is, we are made holy with God's very essence. The sanctification of the Spirit is not an outward change but an inward addition of God's very essence into our being. A mortuary has the job of making dead persons look good outwardly. That is an outward beautification that has nothing to do with life. Our conduct, or our outward beauty, must be an expression of the inward life. The sanctification of the Holy Spirit is not something outward but something absolutely inward of life.

THE ANOINTING SPIRIT

The Spirit of life is also the anointing Spirit (1 John 2:27). The Spirit of life is liberating, transforming, renewing, sanctifying, and anointing. The anointing is the moving and working of the indwelling, all-inclusive life-giving Spirit. The Spirit anoints us with all the divine elements of the Divine

Trinity. The anointing is like the repeated painting of some article. When coat after coat of paint is added to something, the elements of the paint are added to the thing painted. The Holy Spirit anoints us with the divine paint, with Christ, the embodiment of the Triune God. The anointing of the Holy Spirit is not merely a cleansing but a painting of the divine elements of Christ into our being. God's desire is to add Himself into us, to dispense Himself into us. While the Holy Spirit is anointing us, He kills the negative things in our being, and He purifies and cleanses us with all that Christ is.

The holy anointing ointment in Exodus 30:23-25 is a full type of the compound Spirit of God with which we are anointed. The ingredients of this ointment include all that Christ is, all that Christ has accomplished, all that Christ has attained, and all that Christ has obtained. This all-inclusive, compound ointment is the very paint with which the Holy Spirit paints us. All the ingredients of the compound ointment are the essence of Christ as the embodiment of the Triune God. The more the Holy Spirit anoints us, the more we become the same as Christ in life and in nature.

If we want to change the color of a dark house to green, we need to paint it with green paint. We are like a dark house, and Christ is the green paint. Green signifies God's rich life. The more the Holy Spirit anoints us with Christ, the more we become the same as Christ and the more we become Christ. We become Christ because the essence and the element of Christ have been anointed into us, have been added into us. The anointing is altogether a matter in life.

THE STRENGTHENING SPIRIT

Ephesians 3:16 says that we need to be strengthened into our inner man through the Spirit. Many times when I am hungry, I feel weak, so I need to eat some food to be strengthened. I feel weak because I am empty within. I need the inner strengthening. After eating a good meal, I am fully strengthened and energized from within. Physically, we need to be strengthened by taking food into our being. Spiritually, we need to be strengthened into our inner man with Christ through the Holy Spirit. The Holy Spirit brings more and more of Christ into our inner man, and we are energized and strengthened. This means that we gain more life supply.

In 1948 I was laboring in Brother Watchman Nee's hometown of Foochow, which was a place famous for producing oranges. I stayed there for about three weeks and labored day and night in the Lord's work. When I became tired after a meeting, I would drink a glass of fresh orange juice; within a short period of time, I was energized, strengthened, and refreshed. In the same way that our physical being receives the life supply from orange juice, we need the life supply of the Spirit, the inner strengthening of the Spirit. Many times we may feel weak or depressed. At these times we need to open ourselves to the Lord and say, "O Lord, Amen."

We need to learn to breathe in the Lord deeply from within. When we breathe in the Lord, we can sense the inner strengthening and energizing of the Holy Spirit. When we call on the Lord, the Holy Spirit strengthens us with Christ as the life supply. I cannot define the elements that are within a glass of fresh orange juice, but I can enjoy its nourishment and refreshment. There is some element in the orange juice that nourishes, energizes, strengthens, and refreshes. There are also some real, divine, heavenly, spiritual elements in the breath of the Holy Spirit. When we breathe Him in, we get strengthened into our inner man.

The more that we are transformed, renewed, sanctified, anointed, and strengthened by the Spirit, the more life supply we enjoy and the more growth in life we will have. The husky and tall American men have grown in their human life because they have enjoyed the riches of America. Likewise, our spiritual weight and growth in life come from the riches of Christ. As the Spirit of Christ daily liberates, transforms, renews, sanctifies, and anoints us, He adds Christ into us so that we gain an additional weight of Christ. This addition of Christ into our being issues in our growth in life.

By taking in all the rich food of America, an American child will grow and be changed metabolically over a period of time. As the Spirit of Christ adds Christ into our being, we grow and are transformed metabolically. The Spirit liberates, transforms, renews, sanctifies, and anoints us for the one purpose of putting Christ into us so that He can be the very element of our inward being. We need to cooperate with the Spirit of life, who is dispensing more and more of Christ into us little by little in many ways. We are not interested in mere teachings, because teachings can never replace the ingredients of Christ Himself. We trust in the life-giving Spirit because this Spirit works to liberate us, transform us, renew us, sanctify us, and anoint us, bringing Christ into us and adding Christ into us little by little and day by day. As we cooperate with the work of the life-giving Spirit, we are increasing in the riches of Christ, and we are gaining more life so that we can grow in life.

THE FRUIT OF THE SPIRIT

Galatians 5:22 refers to the fruit of the Spirit. Fruit is the expression and the outflow of the inner life. Out of the inward renewing of the Spirit comes the fruit of the Spirit. As Christ is added into our being through the transforming, sanctifying, and anointing Spirit, the fruit of the Spirit will come forth from us. This fruit is the outward expression of the inward working of the Spirit, which is the Spirit's renewing. The more we are renewed, transformed, sanctified, and anointed by the Holy Spirit, the more fruit we will bear of the Spirit. The Spirit brings forth fruit full of life through our inward enjoyment of Christ.

The fruit of the Spirit is singular, but the expression of the fruit is listed in Galatians 5:22-23 with nine items as illustrations. The fruit of the Spirit has other aspects, but only these nine are listed in Galatians 5. The fruit of the Spirit is Christ Himself in many aspects expressed in love, joy, peace, long-suffering, kindness, goodness, faithfulness, meekness, and self-control. This fruit of the Spirit is the one Christ expressed in many aspects. The fruit brought forth by the Spirit is simply Christ. When Christ is brought into us, He is the nourishment. When Christ is brought forth out of us, He is the fruit. The working of the Spirit of life is to bring Christ into us and to bring forth Christ out of us. The fruit of the Spirit is absolutely a matter of life.

LIVING BY THE SPIRIT

To live by the Spirit is to have our life dependent upon and regulated by the Spirit. To live by the Spirit in Galatians 5:25 equals to walk by the Spirit in verse 16. To live by the Spirit, to walk by the Spirit, is a matter of life. Living by the Spirit is not a matter merely of outward behavior or conduct but is an inward matter of life. To live does not mean to act. Many times parents tell their children to behave themselves. For the children to behave themselves is to act in a way that may be different from what they are. It is possible for a monkey to be trained to act like a man. I once saw a demonstration of a monkey who was trained to eat food with a fork. He was dressed with a little cap on his head and a jacket, and he was trained to walk on two feet instead of four. After the demonstration, the monkey began to behave the way he normally did. He took off the cap and the jacket, threw away the fork, and began to walk on all fours. He was taught to behave, or act, like a man, but in his being he was still a monkey. We Christians should not be ones who act or behave in a way that is different from our being. We need to live by the Spirit.

Many of us may behave, or act, in a Christian meeting. Outside of the meeting we may live in a different way. Just like the monkey who behaved like a man, we may behave like a "man" in the meetings and like a "monkey" outside the meetings. This is wrong. We Christians should not be those who act or who try to behave ourselves. We need to be those who live by the Spirit, who walk by the Spirit. We should not live by ourselves, by our old man, but we need to live by the Spirit.

THE SPIRIT OF REALITY

The book of John refers to the Spirit of reality (14:17; 16:13). The reality is Christ (14:6). In the entire universe Christ is the one reality of all. The real light is Christ. The love that we have is not the real love. The real love is Christ. The Bible tells us to honor our parents, and we need to realize that the real honor is Christ. If we do not have Christ, we cannot have the real honor to our parents. The real honesty is Christ. The real patience is Christ. Our patience is not the real patience because after a certain amount of testing, our patience is gone. Our patience is limited, but Christ as patience is unlimited because He is the real patience. Christ is the reality, and the Spirit of life is also the Spirit of reality. If we have the Spirit of life, we have Christ as reality. Today the Spirit of reality is within us (v. 17). We have to realize this indwelling Spirit of reality in a practical way. Day by day we should be able to testify that the Spirit is so real within us.

In John 16:15 the Lord Jesus said, "All that the Father has is Mine; for this reason I have said that He receives of Mine and will declare it to you." The reality and the fullness of the Father are Christ's. The Father passes on all His riches and His fullness to the Son. Then the Spirit receives all the things from Christ to show us. All that the Father is and has is embodied in the Son (Col. 2:9), and all that the Son is and has is revealed as reality to the believers through the Spirit. What the Spirit shows to us is not a kind of teaching but the things of the Father. The things of the Father are Christ's, and the Spirit receives all the things of the Father from Christ to show us. The reality is the Father's, the Father passes on the reality to the Son, the Spirit receives this reality from the Son, and He shows us this reality. The Spirit of life brings all that God is in Christ to us as the reality. In this reality is all that we need. This reality includes life, light, patience, love, humility, kindness, wisdom, and knowledge.

THE FELLOWSHIP OF THE SPIRIT

Second Corinthians 13:14 says, "The grace of the Lord Jesus Christ and the love of God and the fellowship of the Holy Spirit be with you all." We should not consider this verse merely as a benediction. We should read this verse with a realization of God's economy and of God's dispensing. The love of God is God Himself, the grace of Christ is Christ Himself, and the fellowship of the Spirit is the Spirit Himself. Love is the source, grace is the course, and the fellowship is the flow. In the divine dispensing, God's love as the source is manifested in the grace of Christ as the course and transmitted into us as the fellowship of the Spirit, the flow of the Spirit. The love of God, the grace of Christ, and the fellowship of the Spirit are not three separate matters but three aspects of one thing. As long as we are in the flow of the Spirit, we have the grace of Christ with the love of God. We enjoy the grace of Christ with the love of God in the fellowship of the Spirit, in the flow of the Spirit. This enjoyment of the divine dispensing of the Divine Trinity is absolutely a matter of life.

Second Corinthians 1 tells us that God has anointed us with this Spirit (v. 21); chapter 3 tells us that this Spirit is the Spirit who gives life, liberates, and transforms; and the conclusion of 2 Corinthians tells us that this Spirit is the Spirit of fellowship. The Spirit of fellowship is the Spirit of life who gives life and who anoints, liberates, and transforms us. The Spirit of life communicates and transmits all that God is in Christ into us for our enjoyment so that we may gain God in a full way.

CHAPTER FOURTEEN

SAVED BY LIFE

(1)

Scripture Reading: John 1:4; 10:10b; 11:25; 1 John 5:12; Col. 3:4a; Rom. 5:10, 12, 17-19, 21; 6:4; Phil. 3:10a

We have seen the tree of life, the water of life, the breath of life, the seed of life, and the Spirit of life. In this chapter we come to life itself. Nothing is as hard to define as life.

THE RECORD OF LIFE IN GENESIS 1 AND 2

We should remember that Genesis 1 and 2 are a record of life. There are four categories of life in Genesis 1 and 2: the vegetable life, the animal life, the human life, and the divine life. The vegetable life, the animal life, and the human life are lives created by God. Only the divine life is uncreated and eternal. It is the life from eternity unto eternity. With all the other categories of lives there is a beginning and ending because they are created lives, but only one category of life, one unique life, the divine life of God, is eternal and uncreated with no beginning or ending.

In Genesis 1 and 2 all the lower lives are for the higher lives. The plant life is for the animal life, the animal life is for the human life, and the human life is for the divine life. Only the human life is qualified to be for the divine life. Why is only the human life qualified to contain the divine life? The best illustration of this marvelous divine reality is that of a glove and a hand. A person's hand cannot fit in a handker- chief because it does not have the image or form of the hand. Because a glove is in the image, the likeness, and the form of a hand, it is able to contain the hand. A glove is made in the form of a hand for the purpose of containing the hand. The human life was created according to the likeness of the divine life so that God could dispense Himself as the divine life into the human life. Only the human life is qualified to contain the divine life because the human life is in the likeness of the divine life. God created us in His likeness because His purpose was that we would contain Him. To fulfill this purpose, God created us with a human spirit. Our human spirit is the organ for us to receive God and contain God. Thus, the human spirit is the means and the organ to fulfill God's divine purpose.

THE REAL LIFE BEING THE DIVINE LIFE

The vegetable life, the animal life, and the human life are not the real life. They are shadows, figures, or pictures of the real life, the divine life. They show forth different aspects of the unique life, the divine life. The beauty of certain flowers points to the beauty of the divine life. The divine life is actually more beautiful than anything that can be seen in the plant life. The many fruit trees which bear many types of fruit are a shadow showing us how fruitful the divine life is. The forest, which is full of trees, is a picture of the abundance of the divine life. Furthermore, the human life has the likeness of the divine life. Man's wisdom in scientific endeavors is a picture of the wisdom of the divine life. All the positive attributes, features, and aspects of the vegetable life, animal life, and human life are shadows or pictures of the divine life. According to the divine concept, if we do not have the divine life, we do not have life. The human life that we possess is not the real life but is only a figure, a shadow, of life. We need to have the life that is really life (1 Tim. 6:19). This is why 1 John 5:12 tells us that if we have the Son, we have the life, and if we do not have the Son, we do not have the life.

WHAT LIFE IS

Now we need to ask what life is. Life is God Himself; life is God in Christ; life is God in Christ as the Spirit; life is Christ with God; and life is the Spirit with all the riches of Christ in all the fullness of the Godhead. John 1:4 says,

"In Him was life." The One in whom there is life is the One who was the Word in the beginning, who was with God in the beginning, who was God in the beginning, and through whom all things came into being. In this One was life. This life was the light of men (v. 4). John 10:10b tells us that the Lord Jesus came that we might have life and have it abundantly. This is the purpose of Christ's coming. First Timothy 1:15 says that "Christ Jesus came into the world to save sinners." He came into the world to save us from our sins, to deal with the negative side (Matt. 1:21). The positive purpose of Christ's coming, however, is that we may have life and have it abundantly.

This life is life with resurrection power. The life we have received from God through Christ is a resurrection life. We have to differentiate life from resurrection. Resurrection is life that has been tested by passing through death. The life that we possess is a life with resurrection power. This life has been tested by being put into death and by passing through death. Christ is the resurrection and the life (John 11:25). Because Christ is the resurrection, it was not possible for Him to be held by death (Acts 2:24). Death cannot hold the resurrection life. If we have the Son, we have this life. If we do not have the Son, we do not have this life. Because we have received the Son, we can declare that we have this life. We can say, "Christ our life" (Col. 3:4a).

SAVED IN HIS LIFE

Romans 5:10 says, "If we, being enemies, were reconciled to God through the death of His Son, much more we will be saved in His life, having been reconciled." The two main items in this verse are the death of the Son of God and the life of the Son of God. In addition to the death and the life of the Son of God, there are the two matters of reconciliation and salvation. Reconciliation is through His death. Salvation is in His life. Reconciliation to God through Christ has been accomplished already, but to be saved in His life from many negative things is still a daily matter. We also need to pay attention to the words *much more* in this verse. We have been reconciled, but much more we will be saved in the Lord's life.

As sinners we need justification, but as enemies we need reconciliation. Because of the enmity between us and God, there was the need of reconciliation. We were not only sinners but also enemies. When we were enemies, we were reconciled to God through the death of Christ. We can say that we have been saved from the lake of fire and from God's condemnation through the redeeming blood of Christ. But according to Romans 5:10, we still need to be saved in His life, which is the divine life, the real life.

Saved from the Law of Sin, the Flesh, and Death

After we have been saved from God's condemnation and from the lake of fire, we need to be saved first from the law of sin. The law of sin is the besetting power of sin. Romans 8:2 says that the law of the Spirit of life sets us free from the law of sin. The second item that we need to be saved from is the flesh. The third negative item that we need to be saved from is death. Death includes all negative things. Our sloppiness, looseness, weakness, negative thoughts, and failures are included in death. We need to be saved from the law of sin, from the flesh, and from death. The law of sin, the flesh, and death are prevailing and powerful negative items that trouble us even after we have been regenerated with the divine life. If we are going to know what it is to be saved in His life, we have to be saved from these negative items.

The Definition of Death

Death always goes with sin. Death is the issue of sin. Sin is the cause, and death is the effect. Whenever we have sin, death is there. Death is the shortage of ability to fulfill God's requirements according to His divine standard. God requires that we honor our parents. If we cannot honor our parents, that is death. In the eyes of God, death is with us because we cannot fulfill His requirements. The Lord also tells us, "You shall be holy because I am holy" (1 Pet. 1:16). If we cannot be holy, this means that we are dead. God wants us to be diligent. If we are sloppy, this is death. God requires that we be watchful, but we may always be sleeping. This means that we are short of the ability to fulfill God's requirements and that death is with us. God desires that we be careful persons, but we may be careless day after day. Many young brothers may seem to be living, but actually they are dead because they are short of the ability to fulfill God's requirements according to His divine standard.

The Pattern of the Lord Jesus

From 1920 through 1925, the Lord did something miraculous in China by saving a number of college and high school students. During that time, a real change was taking place in China due to the young generation. Their concept was being revolutionized with the thought that man has to be free. The Chinese people had many teachings, customs, habits, traditions, and regulations. Young people in the early 1920s in China desired to abandon these regulations so that they could be free. In the 1920s in China a young person was required to rise up when an older person entered the room. A teenager did not have the freedom to say anything in the presence of his elders, and he could not sit down until they left his presence. It was under this kind of environment that we young people in China were saved by the Lord. Because of the desire to be free from regulations, some who were saved had the concept that Jesus never regulated others and that He was not under any regulations. To them real freedom meant no regulations. Actually, however, to have no regulations is looseness and death. By reading the Scriptures, we can see that the Lord Jesus was a very careful person. He was neither sloppy nor loose.

The Gospels give us a record of the Lord's feeding five thousand people at one time (Matt. 14:14-21). These people were enjoying the Lord's teaching, but the hour became late, and they became hungry. The disciples asked the Lord to dismiss the people so that they could go and get something to eat. But the Lord charged the disciples, "You give them something to eat" (Mark 6:37). The Gospels record the miracle of the Lord's feeding five thousand with only five loaves and two fish, but we can also see that the Lord did everything in a very careful way and in a good order. The disciples presented the Lord Jesus with the loaves and the fish, and He told the disciples to have the people sit down in companies of hundreds and fifties (John 6:10; cf. Mark 6:39-40). This shows how orderly the Lord Jesus was. Before the people ate, He required that they sit down in an orderly way in companies.

After such a great miracle of feeding the five thousand, the Lord Jesus instructed the disciples to pick up what was left over of the bread and of the fish. Mark 6:43 tells us that the disciples "took up twelve full handbaskets of the broken pieces of bread and of the fish." If we were there with the disciples, we probably would not care about the fragments of bread and of fish. But the Lord Jesus was not careless. When He was on this earth, He was so orderly and did everything in a careful way. God's creation testifies of His orderliness. There is nothing chaotic about God's creation, but everything is in order.

Our Need to Be Saved in His Life

If we are sloppy, careless, or loose, this proves that we cannot fulfill God's requirements according to His divine standard, so death is with us. We need to be saved in His life. We need His life so that we can be living, capable, and full of energy and ability to fulfill God's requirements according to His divine standard. To be living does not mean that we are merely active or lively but that we are able to fulfill God's requirements. It is good for us to say, "Hallelujah! Praise the Lord!" But suppose that God wants us to be quiet. If we cannot be quiet, that means that death is with us. If we are required to be at certain places on time and cannot be there on time, this is death. The shortage of ability to be on time means that death is with us. When the Lord tells us to jump and shout, we should be one with Him. When the Lord wants us to be quiet, we need to be quiet. Our being one with the Lord proves that we are full of life because we are full of the ability and capability to fulfill the Lord's requirements. If we are short of the ability to fulfill God's requirements, that is a strong proof that we are dead. How we all need to be saved in His life!

We need to have some fellowship with the Lord concerning our need to be saved in His life. In our daily life, do we have the ability to fulfill the Lord's requirements? If we do not, we are short of life. A shortage of ability to fulfill the Lord's requirements according to His divine standard means that we are short of life. It means that death is with us and that we need the Lord's life to save us. Much more, we shall be saved in His life. To be saved is not a matter merely of being justified, forgiven by God, and saved from the lake of fire. We need to be saved from the shortage of ability to glorify Him, to please Him, and to fulfill His requirements. We need more life. We need life abundantly. We need to be saved in such a rich way. We need to bring the fellowship in this chapter to the Lord in prayer so that we can be saved in His life in our daily life.

CHAPTER FIFTEEN

SAVED BY LIFE

(2)

Scripture Reading: Rom. 5:10, 12, 17-19, 21; 6:4; Phil. 3:10a

SIN AND DEATH IN ADAM
VERSUS RIGHTEOUSNESS AND LIFE IN CHRIST

Romans 5 shows us two persons—Adam and Christ. The disobedience of one man is versus the obedience of the One (v. 19). Adam is the first man, and Christ is the second man. In the Bible God's desire is with the second man, not the first man. Isaac's two sons were Esau and Jacob. God rejected Esau, the firstborn, and He loved Jacob, the second child (9:13). Also, the book of Exodus tells us that God's ultimate judgment on Egypt was for all the firstborn ones to be killed (11:4-5). The first represents the soulish man, while the second represents the spiritual man (1 Cor. 15:46-47). We were in Adam, the first man, but now we are in Christ, the second man. We were born in Adam, but we have been born the second time in Christ. Our first birth was of Adam, and our second birth was of Christ. Anyone who has had only one birth has not been saved and is not of Christ. Because we have had our first birth in Adam and our second birth in Christ, we are of Christ.

According to Romans 5, we inherited sin and death in Adam (v. 12). Sin brought us under God's condemnation (vv. 16, 18). As long as we are sinful, we are condemned by God under His righteous judgment. Death brings us into a situation where we are absolutely unable to fulfill any of God's requirements. Because we are dead, we do not have the ability to be humble or patient according to God's divine standard. Romans 5 shows us that we were first under a situation in which we were condemned by God, and we were also in a situation in which we were absolutely unable to fulfill God's requirements. Thank God, however, that Christ died for us. His death has solved our first problem. Our being under God's condemnation is now absolutely over. But today we are still, in a sense, in the second situation of not being able to fulfill God's requirements.

From Adam we inherited sin and death. From Christ we received righteousness and life (vv. 17-19). Righteousness and life are the two main items we have received in and of Christ. Righteousness is versus sin, and life is versus death. We inherited sin, but we have received righteousness. Righteousness canceled sin. We inherited death from Adam, but we have received life in Christ. Life cancels and swallows up death. Righteousness in Christ is related to His death. Life in Christ is related to His resurrection. He died for our sin, and He was resurrected for us to have life. His death solves the problem of our sin, and His resurrection imparts to us His life in order to vanquish and to swallow up death. On the one hand, we have been reconciled to God by His death. On the other hand, we are now being saved in His life from death. Death is our problem. Having been reconciled, much more we will be saved in His life from death (v. 10), which is the inability and disability to fulfill God's requirements according to His divine standard.

FREEDOM IN CHRIST VERSUS LOOSENESS

We have to apply this fellowship to our practical daily life. Sloppiness, looseness, and carelessness are weaknesses, and weaknesses are different aspects of death. We are sloppy, loose, and careless because we are weak, and all the weaknesses are aspects of death. We may have the thought that if we could have more freedom, that would be wonderful. But the kind of freedom that we desire may not actually be freedom but looseness.

We have to differentiate freedom from looseness. Looseness is a condition of our daily life in which we cannot help ourselves. We may not be able to help ourselves get to bed at the right time. We may not be able to help ourselves keep things in order. When we are strong and sober in our mentality, spontaneously we are not so loose. When the time comes that we need to smile, we should be able to smile. When the time comes that we need to weep, we should weep. When the time comes that we need to laugh, we should laugh. Looseness means that there is no control. Looseness is death. Freedom is not being under the bondage of anything. When we are free, we do what we feel that we have to do. Freedom is to laugh when we feel we have to laugh and to stop laughing when we feel that we need to stop. When we are free, we are not under the bondage of anything.

We are able to regulate ourselves when we are enjoying real freedom. Our being able to manage a car that we are driving means that we are driving the car in freedom. We can use the brakes when we have to, and we can step on the gas when we have to. To drive in a condition of looseness would mean that the brake or the steering wheel on the car did not work. The real freedom in driving is that the car is absolutely under our control. We need to live a sound, sober, and normal life, and that life is Christ. Christ is so sound, sober, normal, and strong.

THE REGULATED HUMAN LIVING OF CHRIST

The four Gospels unveil the marvelous humanity of the Lord Jesus. What a marvelous daily life and human living He had when He was on this earth! He was a person who was noble, solid, sober, and proper in every way. The Gospel of John unveils the Lord Jesus as the very God who passed through human living on this earth. The book of John shows us in particular how the Lord Jesus as life meets the need of every man's case.

John 11 shows us that the need of the dead is life's resurrecting. In this chapter we can see the Lord Jesus' marvelous divine humanity. The Scriptures tell us that Jesus loved Mary and Martha and their brother Lazarus (v. 5). One day Lazarus became very ill, and Martha and Mary sent the news to the Lord Jesus. When the Lord Jesus heard that

Lazarus was sick, He stayed in the place where He was for another two days (v. 6). He had the full freedom to go to visit Lazarus or not to go. The "brake" of His "car" was so workable.

The disciples were people who were easily moved, but the Lord Jesus was so stable. When the news came about Lazarus's sickness, the Lord's heart was not moved. The disciples must have been puzzled and perplexed. You can imagine how disappointed they were. After two days the Lord suddenly expressed a desire to see Lazarus. When the Lord did not want to go, they were puzzled, and when the Lord was ready to go, they thought that it was not necessary to go. They said to the Lord, "Rabbi, the Jews were just now seeking to stone You, and You are going there again?" (v. 8). What the Lord would not do, the disciples would do, and what the Lord would do, the disciples would not agree with. We may say that the reason for this is because they did not know the will of God. But we must also see that the disciples were not so normal. They were people who were easily excited and offended.

If we are easily offended, this means that we are not so normal. If we could be rebuked and scorned severely without being offended, this shows that we have the real freedom. Sometimes, however, just a single word can offend us. We are easily offended because we are weak and full of death. If we easily misunderstand others and are easily offended and unhappy with others, this proves that we are weak and dead. We do not have the life power to manage ourselves. When the disciples did go with the Lord to visit Lazarus, they went reluctantly. Even Thomas said to the other disciples, "Let us also go, that we may die with Him" (v. 16).

When the Lord Jesus was on His way to the village at Bethany, the first one who came to meet Him was Martha. Martha said to the Lord Jesus, "If You had been here, my brother would not have died" (v. 21). Then the Lord Jesus told Martha that her brother would rise again and that He is the resurrection and the life (vv. 23, 25). But Martha did not hear what the Lord Jesus said. Her response was that she knew that her brother would rise again in the resurrection in the last day (v. 24). After her conversation with the Lord

Jesus, Martha went away and told her sister Mary that the Lord was there and that He was calling her (v. 28). This was Martha's opinion and not the Lord's command. The Lord Jesus was not offended by the opinions of Martha, Mary (v. 32), and the Jews (vv. 36-37). At one point, the Lord wept in sympathy with their sorrow over Lazarus's death. In John 11 we can see that the Lord was always in full control of Himself. With Him there was the full freedom. He was absolutely free, and there was not one bit of looseness with Him because He was full of life.

ENJOYING CHRIST
AS THE DIVINE INNER LIFE
FOR A PROPER HUMAN LIVING

If I laugh or weep without limitation and without control, that means I am full of death. We have to realize that if we partake of Christ and enjoy Him as our life, our whole being, our whole human living, will be absolutely changed. Our partaking of the transforming life of Christ will not only enable us to overcome some sins and besetting habits but will also and more importantly swallow up all the death of our natural man to make us absolutely another person. Then when we laugh, we will laugh in a different way. When we weep, we will weep in a way full of control. We may be happy and excited, but we will be happy and excited under a certain control. When every part of our being is under the control and inner regulation of Christ as the divine inner life, this is the real freedom.

Lawlessness and looseness are not freedom. Freedom is to be under the full control of the divine life yet without bondage. Our being able to do household duties at the proper times with joy is a proof that we have the life power within us. The life power within us enables us to wash the dishes, to be on time, and to get to bed at the proper time. Doing these things will not be a bondage but a joy if we are enjoying the real freedom in the divine life. We need to enjoy the life power, the power of the Lord's resurrection, to have a proper human living in our daily life. Nothing should be a bondage, a pressure, or a suffering to us, but in everything we should have the joy of the Lord because we are being saved in His life. If we do not have the life, whatever we do will be a pressure or a suffering. We need the real experience of Christ as our inner saving life.

LIFE FOR THE BUILDING UP OF THE BODY

Much more, we will be saved in His life from death. This kind of saving from death includes being set free from sin and also includes sanctification, transformation, conformation to the image of Christ, and the building up of the Body. We are independent because we are short of life. In Ezekiel 37 the bones were dried up thoroughly, so every bone was individual and separate from the other bones. The bones were separated and detached from one another because there was no life. Because there was no life, they were disjointed, separated, and absolutely individualistic. The bones of our human body are joined together to be one body through, by, and with life. In like manner, we are built together into one Body through, by, and with the divine life.

THE TRANSFORMATION AND GROWTH OF LIFE

We need to be impressed that in many respects we are still full of death. We are still so weak, loose, sloppy, careless, independent, individualistic, and unwilling to be coordinated with others. All these are signs of our weakness, and our weakness is simply deadness. We need the divine life. The more life we have, the more this life will swallow up the death in our being. Then there will be a real transformation in us.

Do not think that transformation is something that happens in a sudden way. Transformation goes on hour after hour, moment by moment, and little by little all day long. By the Lord's mercy, I have been under the transformation of the inner life for many years. We should not think that it is necessary to pray and fast for a period of time to undergo the process of transformation. Transformation does not come in a sudden way but works in a very normal way day by day. Bit by bit the transformation of the inner life works in a very normal and ordinary way, even with the small things in our daily life. We may not be able to sense the transformation of life, but after a certain period of time there will be a difference in our being because of the growth of life.

We cannot see much growth in life in a young child from day to day, but after a year we are able to see some growth in life. From one day to the next we cannot see any difference in the flowers or fruit trees. But after a certain period of time, we are able to see the flowers blossom and the fruit trees bear fruit. The growth of the plant life is not something that comes suddenly but gradually. After a certain period of time, we are able to see the blossoms and the fruit, the evidence of the growth of life.

If we mean business with the Lord to enjoy Christ as the life within us, there should be a change with us after a certain period of time. If there is no change or progress with us after a certain amount of time, this indicates that we are not enjoying the saving inner life of Christ. The more that we say, "O Lord, Amen," the more life we will receive. Spontaneously, we will be saved in His life from all the signs of death. We will be saved from all the weakness and inability to meet God's requirements according to His divine standard.

KNOWING THE POWER OF
THE LORD'S RESURRECTION LIFE

In Philippians 3:10a Paul said that he wanted to know the power of the Lord's resurrection. This power is His resurrection life which raised Him from among the dead (Eph. 1:19-20). We need to know and experience the life power of the Lord's resurrection to be saved in His life.

SAVED IN LIFE TO REIGN IN LIFE AND
BE BUILT UP INTO THE BODY OF CHRIST

We need to bring this fellowship to the Lord and pray-read the verses in the Scripture reading in Romans until we sense that the life within us is really ruling and reigning like a king. Then we will not only walk in newness of life (6:4) and not only be saved in life (5:10), but we will also reign in life (v. 17). Then we will have the full freedom. We will reign as a king in life by taking Christ as life. Nothing will be a bondage to us because we will be free in our enjoyment of the saving life of Christ. As we are being saved in His life, we will be sanctified, transformed, and built up into the Body of Christ. Sanctification, transformation, and the building up of the Body come out of the saving of life.

THE WAY TO ENJOY THE SAVING OF LIFE

The way that we enjoy this saving of life is revealed in Romans 10. Verses 12 and 13 tell us that the Lord is rich to all who call upon Him and that whoever calls upon the name of the Lord shall be saved. When we call upon the name of the Lord, we are saved in His life. When we call upon Him, we enjoy the saving life. May the Lord be merciful to us so that we may enjoy His saving life to the fullest extent day by day.

CHAPTER SIXTEEN

THE DEVELOPMENT OF LIFE

Scripture Reading: 2 Pet. 1:1-11; 3:18

In the previous chapters we have seen something concerning the matter of life in the writings of John and Paul. The main ministries in the New Testament are those of John, Paul, and Peter, and the teaching in the New Testament is mainly based upon the writings of these three apostles. John's writings occupy the beginning and end of the New Testament; the Gospel of John is at the beginning, and the book of Revelation is at the end. John stresses life and opens the way for life in his Gospel. He also ends with the matter of life in the book of Revelation. All of the apostles stressed the matter of life. Each of them had their unique way to present the same one thing—life. In this chapter we want to see Peter's marvelous presentation of the divine life in his second Epistle.

THREE GREAT ITEMS GIVEN TO US BY GOD

According to 2 Peter 1:1-4 there are three great items which have been given to us by God: equally precious faith, the divine power, and the precious and exceedingly great promises. Faith is not of our works, nor of our endeavor or strife, but is God's allotted gift to us (v. 1). God has also given us the divine power, which is the power of the divine life related to the divine nature. Furthermore, because God has called us to His own glory and virtue, He has given us His precious and exceedingly great promises to assure us, encourage us, strengthen us, and speed us on our way toward this goal.

Equally Precious Faith

God has allotted us, that is, given to us, equally precious faith. More than forty years ago I wrote a note alongside this verse in one of my Bibles, which says, "Although I cannot compare with the apostle Peter, I have something which is exactly the same as what he has—equally precious faith." We have received this faith; it did not originate with us.

It is difficult to say what faith is, but it is very precious to us. Although faith is hard to define, we can say that we have it and that we cannot lose it. Faith has been put into us by God. Whether we are strong or weak, whether we stand or fall, from the day we received the Lord Jesus, faith remains with us always. Some young people, after receiving the Lord Jesus, may regret and wish that they could not believe anymore. Nevertheless, because they have believed into the Lord and have been captured by Him, they cannot get away from Him. They have been "hooked" by Christ. To believe is easy, but after believing, it is very difficult not to believe. A person can leave mere teaching or even disregard the Bible, but he cannot throw away this faith. This faith always remains with us and unconditionally binds us to Christ. Once we have it, we cannot lose it. This is why this faith is so precious. Faith is a seed sown into us which is divine and eternal. This faith is the foundation, the root, and the seed of our Christian life.

The Divine Power

God has also given us the marvelous and mysterious divine power. God as the divine power passed through creation, redemption, and resurrection to become the life-giving Spirit (1 Cor. 15:45b). This divine power is nothing less than the life-giving Spirit, who is God Himself as life to us in resurrection. The visible things of the creation came into being through God's divine power. Redemption was also accomplished by God's divine power. The one man Jesus could die on behalf of all men to accomplish an eternal redemption (Heb. 9:12) because of the divine power. Today as the life-giving Spirit, He offers Himself to us as the divine power in resurrection. When we receive the Lord Jesus, the very Triune God enters into us as life in resurrection. This life in resurrection is the divine power, which is God Himself as the life-giving Spirit.

The divine power in 2 Peter 1:3 is the power of the divine life, and this divine life power has given us all things that relate to life and godliness. The things that relate to life are inexhaustible. They include the law of life (Rom. 8:2; Heb. 8:10), humility, wisdom, rejoicing, love, joy, hope, submission, goodness, meekness, kindness, long-suffering, and peace. Everything related to life has been given to us. The life power within the seed of a certain plant includes everything related to the plant. The life power within the seed includes the stem, branches, leaves, blossoms, flowers, and fruit of the plant. Within the power of the divine life as the seed in us are all the things necessary for the growth of the divine life. In the divine power are virtues such as love, patience, humility, kindness, and long-suffering. The divine power, the power of life, includes all things needed not only for life inwardly but also for godliness outwardly.

Precious and
Exceedingly Great Promises

The third category of great things given to us by God is the precious and exceedingly great promises. The promises in 2 Peter 1:4 are mainly related to our spiritual life. These are promises for the inner life and the outward expression of life. One such promise is in Ephesians 3:20, which says, "To Him who is able to do superabundantly above all that we ask or think, according to the power which operates in us." This promise to do above all that we ask or think is not concerning the material things of the present life but concerning the spiritual things for the church life. The Lord is going to do superabundantly above all that we ask or think for the church life, according to the inner working power that operates in us. Other precious and exceedingly great promises are in Matthew 28:20; John 6:57; 7:38-39; 10:28-29; 14:19-20, 23; 15:5; and 16:13-15.

FIVE GROUPS OF THINGS
FOR THE EXPERIENCE OF LIFE

After the basic categories of faith, the divine power, and the precious promises, there are also five groups of things for the experience of life in 2 Peter. First, we have all things that relate to life and godliness. Life is within, while godliness is without. Life is the inward substance, and godliness is the outward expression. *Godliness,* according to its New Testament usage, refers to our Christian living, our Christian daily walk. It is the outward expression of the inward life. It is a living that is the expression of God (1 Tim. 2:2). Godliness is God-likeness. The Christian life should be a life which expresses God and bears God's likeness in all things. The divine power has given to us all things relating to our inward life and our outward living.

Second, through the promises we become the partakers, or enjoyers, of the divine nature (2 Pet. 1:4). Third, there are the spiritual virtues (vv. 5-7), which are the issue of the development of the divine life. These divine virtues are virtue, knowledge, self-control, endurance, godliness, brotherly love, and love. Fourth, God has called us not merely by His gospel, His grace, or His mercy, but He has called us by His own glory and virtue (v. 3). Fifth, there is the entrance into the eternal kingdom of Jesus Christ. Second Peter 1:11 says, "In this way the entrance into the eternal kingdom of our Lord and Savior Jesus Christ will be richly and bountifully supplied to you." The entrance is conditional; it will be supplied based upon certain terms and conditions.

ADDING ALL DILIGENCE

In 2 Peter 1:5 Peter says, "For this very reason also, adding all diligence, supply bountifully in your faith..." The word *supply* in this verse can also mean "develop." *Develop* is a better word because it implies growth. When a seed grows, it first develops the stem, then the branches, the blossom, and ultimately the fruit. We must develop seven items: in faith develop virtue, in virtue develop knowledge, in knowledge develop self-control, in self-control develop endurance, in endurance develop godliness, in godliness develop brotherly love, and in brotherly love develop love.

We have faith within us as the seed, we have the divine power, and we have the holy Word with its promises. Now based upon what God has given, Peter says that we must add all diligence. The manna in the wilderness is a good illustration of our need to cooperate with God's giving (Exo. 16:4-5, 14-15, 21). Manna came each morning and had to be gathered early because it melted when the sun became hot. The manna was sent by God, but the children of Israel had to exercise themselves diligently to rise up early to go out and gather the manna. God could send the manna to the earth, but He would not put the manna directly into the mouths of the children of Israel. The children of Israel had to do their part. God is gracious, yet regardless of how gracious He is and how sufficient His grace is, we still need to exercise ourselves. The children of Israel not only had to gather the manna, but they also had to take it home and cook it (Num. 11:8; Exo. 16:23). God sent the manna, but He would not cook it for them.

God has given, but we must cooperate with His giving. Second Corinthians 9:10 says, "Now He who bountifully supplies seed to the sower and bread for food will supply and multiply your seed and cause the fruits of righteousness to increase." God gives the seed and the fruit, and in between the seed and the fruit is much development. The development between the seed and the fruit is our responsibility. God gives the seed, but He would not sow the seed or till the ground. To sow the seed and till the ground is our part. Thus, Peter charges us to develop something out of the seed that we already have. On His part God has given us many exceedingly great things. Now we must do our part by adding all diligence. In Genesis 2:5 God did not send the rain, because there was no man to work the ground. God's part needs our part. God has done His part, and now we must do our part to cooperate with Him.

THE SECRETS OF LIFE

Peter's word is very mysterious, yet in this mysterious word are the secrets of life. The first secret is that all things relating to life and godliness are given to us as the seed of faith (2 Pet. 1:1, 3, 5). God has also given us all the promises. He not only gives us the seed and promises the rain, but He also causes the growth (1 Cor. 3:6) and the harvest (2 Cor. 9:10).

The second secret is that, realizing that God has given us everything, we must cooperate with God to do our part. God promises to do more, yet this promise is conditional, depending upon what we do. Many of the great promises are conditional. If we do something, then God will do something more. If we sow the seed, God will give the bread. If we sow the seed, God will send the rain. The further giving by God depends upon our cooperation. If we do not sow or till the earth, then there will be no rain, no growth, and no harvest.

The third secret of life is that, as we cooperate with God, we should not do anything outside of what He has given. We must develop what He has given. God has given us the seed. We must do everything to develop the seed by preparing the soil, sowing the seed, and watering the seed.

Second Peter 1:4 says, "Through which He has granted to us precious and exceedingly great promises that through these you might become partakers of the divine nature." Here the fourth secret of life is shown. By partaking of the divine nature through the precious promises, we develop virtue, knowledge, self-control, endurance, godliness, brotherly love, and love by the growth in life (vv. 5-7). The precious promises are embodied in the divine word. By pray-reading the promises, we partake of and enjoy the divine nature, and by partaking of the divine nature, we develop in life. The more we pray-read the promises, the more we enjoy the divine nature, and the more we enjoy the divine nature, the more we grow and develop in life.

We must develop the faith within us. First, in our faith we must develop virtue. Virtue is the explanation of the excellencies of Christ. First Peter 2:9 refers to the virtues, or excellencies, of Christ. Virtue is the excellency of Christ expressed through us. It is the excellent expression of Christ. When anything of Christ is expressed through us, that is something excellent, and this excellency is virtue.

We can realize a kind of excellency with many brothers and sisters. With one brother, we may realize the patience of Christ. With a certain sister, we may realize the humility of Christ. These virtues are the excellent expression of Christ. We have faith as the seed within us. Now this seed needs further development and expression. This expression is virtue. According to my realization and experience, virtue means the expression of Christ. We must develop the expression of Christ in our faith. Our virtue is the expression of Christ in our daily life.

Virtue is a kind of power, the excellency which comes out of Christ. Mark 5:30 says, "Immediately Jesus realizing in Himself that power had gone out of Him, turned around in the crowd and said, Who touched My garments?" Luke 6:19 says, "All the crowd sought to touch Him, because power was going out from Him and healing all." Then in Luke 8:46 the Lord Jesus says, "Someone touched Me; for I perceived that power had gone out from Me." In these portions *power* may be translated as "virtue" (KJV).

In virtue we must develop knowledge. Knowledge comes after virtue. If knowledge came before virtue, it would become a frustration to virtue. We need virtue to be developed first, then for further development of virtue, we need knowledge, the proper knowledge. *Knowledge* in 2 Peter 1:6 refers to the knowledge of Christ, that is, the knowing of Christ in a full and excellent way. The last verse of this book confirms this by saying, "Grow in the grace and knowledge of our Lord and Savior Jesus Christ" (3:18). The full knowledge of Jesus Christ, knowing Christ in a deeper and fuller way, helps us to grow and develop. After knowledge, we must develop self-control. Self-control is a restriction. Self-control is toward ourselves, while endurance is toward situations and circumstances. Toward ourselves we need self-control, toward the environment we need endurance, toward God we need godliness, toward the brothers we need brotherly love, and toward the highest needs we need love, the nobler love. Faith is the seed, and love is the harvest. From faith to love there are seven stages of development by the growth in life.

The fifth secret revealed in 2 Peter 1 is that by enjoying

the divine nature, we enter into the kingdom of the Lord Jesus Christ (v. 11). To enter into the kingdom is a matter of growth. While we are growing, we are entering. The more we grow, the more entrance we gain. To enter into the kingdom of the Lord Jesus, we need to grow. If we reach the last step of development, we are fully in the kingdom. We should not think that if we are idle with no development after we are saved, we will enter into the kingdom of Christ. If we have this thought, we will be cheated. To enter into the kingdom is different from salvation. To enter into the kingdom we need the maturity of life, the full growth of life.

DEVELOPMENT BY GROWTH IN LIFE
UNTO THE RICH ENTRANCE
INTO THE ETERNAL KINGDOM

We have seen three main items in 2 Peter 1: the seed of faith, the divine power, which is the growing power, and the precious promises. God has given the seed, the growing power, and the promises that He will send the rain, the growth, and the harvest if we cooperate with Him. With God's giving, we must be diligent to develop the seed of faith by taking the promises, by picking up His word. The best way to pick up His word is to pray-read the word. The more we pray-read all the promises, the more we enjoy the divine nature. As we enjoy this divine nature, we have the growth in life, the maturity in life, and the harvest of life. This maturity is the entrance into the kingdom of the Lord Jesus. We all need to grow in the grace and knowledge of the Lord Jesus Christ.

Second Peter is a book on growth. Its last verse ends in this way: "Grow in the grace..." Chapter 1 reveals the way to grow. We have the seed, the growing power, and the promises that God will send the rain, cause the growth, and give the harvest. Now we need to develop the seed by taking His promises, by pray-reading the word of His promises, that we may enjoy His divine nature. By this we will be developed and grow step by step until we reach maturity. Then we will enjoy a rich entrance into the eternal kingdom of our Lord and Savior Jesus Christ.

ABOUT THE AUTHOR

Witness Lee was born in 1905 in northern China and raised in a Christian family. At age 19 he was fully captured for Christ and immediately consecrated himself to preach the gospel for the rest of his life. Early in his service, he met Watchman Nee, a renowned preacher, teacher, and writer. Witness Lee labored together with Watchman Nee under his direction. In 1934 Watchman Nee entrusted Witness Lee with the responsibility for his publication operation, called the Shanghai Gospel Bookroom.

Prior to the Communist takeover in 1949, Witness Lee was sent by Watchman Nee and his other co-workers to Taiwan to ensure that the things delivered to them by the Lord would not be lost. Watchman Nee instructed Witness Lee to continue the former's publishing operation abroad as the Taiwan Gospel Bookroom, which has been publicly recognized as the publisher of Watchman Nee's works outside China. Witness Lee's work in Taiwan manifested the Lord's abundant blessing. From a mere 350 believers, newly fled from the mainland, the churches in Taiwan grew to 20,000 in five years.

In 1962 Witness Lee felt led of the Lord to come to the United States, settling in California. During his 35 years of service in the U.S., he ministered in weekly meetings and weekend conferences, delivering several thousand spoken messages. Much of his speaking has since been published as over 400 titles. Many of these have been translated into over fourteen languages. He gave his last public conference in February 1997 at the age of 91.

He leaves behind a prolific presentation of the truth in the Bible. His major work, *Life-study of the Bible,* comprises over 25,000 pages of commentary on every book of the Bible from the perspective of the believers' enjoyment and experience of God's divine life in Christ through the Holy Spirit. Witness Lee was the chief editor of a new translation of the New Testament into Chinese called the Recovery Version and directed the translation of the same into English. The Recovery Version also appears in a number of other languages. He provided an extensive body of footnotes, outlines, and spiritual cross references. A radio broadcast of his messages can be heard on Christian radio stations in the United States. In 1965 Witness Lee founded Living Stream Ministry, a non-profit corporation, located in Anaheim, California, which officially presents his and Watchman Nee's ministry.

Witness Lee's ministry emphasizes the experience of Christ as life and the practical oneness of the believers as the Body of Christ. Stressing the importance of attending to both these matters, he led the churches under his care to grow in Christian life and function. He was unbending in his conviction that God's goal is not narrow sectarianism but the Body of Christ. In time, believers began to meet simply as the church in their localities in response to this conviction. In recent years a number of new churches have been raised up in Russia and in many eastern European countries.

OTHER BOOKS PUBLISHED BY
Living Stream Ministry

Titles by Witness Lee:

Abraham—Called by God	978-0-7363-0359-0
The Experience of Life	978-0-87083-417-2
The Knowledge of Life	978-0-87083-419-6
The Tree of Life	978-0-87083-300-7
The Economy of God	978-0-87083-415-8
The Divine Economy	978-0-87083-268-0
God's New Testament Economy	978-0-87083-199-7
The World Situation and God's Move	978-0-87083-092-1
Christ vs. Religion	978-0-87083-010-5
The All-inclusive Christ	978-0-87083-020-4
Gospel Outlines	978-0-87083-039-6
Character	978-0-87083-322-9
The Secret of Experiencing Christ	978-0-87083-227-7
The Life and Way for the Practice of the Church Life	978-0-87083-785-2
The Basic Revelation in the Holy Scriptures	978-0-87083-105-8
The Crucial Revelation of Life in the Scriptures	978-0-87083-372-4
The Spirit with Our Spirit	978-0-87083-798-2
Christ as the Reality	978-0-87083-047-1
The Central Line of the Divine Revelation	978-0-87083-960-3
The Full Knowledge of the Word of God	978-0-87083-289-5
Watchman Nee—A Seer of the Divine Revelation ...	978-0-87083-625-1

Titles by Watchman Nee:

How to Study the Bible	978-0-7363-0407-8
God's Overcomers	978-0-7363-0433-7
The New Covenant	978-0-7363-0088-9
The Spiritual Man • 3 volumes	978-0-7363-0269-2
Authority and Submission	978-0-7363-0185-5
The Overcoming Life	978-1-57593-817-2
The Glorious Church	978-0-87083-745-6
The Prayer Ministry of the Church	978-0-87083-860-6
The Breaking of the Outer Man and the Release ...	978-1-57593-955-1
The Mystery of Christ	978-1-57593-954-4
The God of Abraham, Isaac, and Jacob	978-0-87083-932-0
The Song of Songs	978-0-87083-872-9
The Gospel of God • 2 volumes	978-1-57593-953-7
The Normal Christian Church Life	978-0-87083-027-3
The Character of the Lord's Worker	978-1-57593-322-1
The Normal Christian Faith	978-0-87083-748-7
Watchman Nee's Testimony	978-0-87083-051-8

Available at
Christian bookstores, or contact Living Stream Ministry
2431 W. La Palma Ave. • Anaheim, CA 92801
1-800-549-5164 • www.livingstream.com